Remy slid his hand along the back of the sofa

The move was a sinuous caress, one that made Jade's blood hum even as part of her remained professional and objective.

"You're actually very easy to read, you know," he said.

Jade snorted in disbelief.

"But then maybe it's just our unexpected connection that has your thoughts displayed so plainly."

"What unexpected connection?"

"The fact that I'd much rather get you in bed than investigate my own shooting." He looked inviting as sin. "I assume the sentiment is returned?"

"It hardly matters. We're both professionals, so we're not going to do anything about it."

He smiled, his gaze locking with hers. "Aren't we?"

Blaze™

Dear Reader,

Big confession time—I don't know how to steal artwork. I'm not really crazy about guns. I love jeans but don't own a kick-ass pair of green alligator boots (as much as I'd like to). I can't circumvent sophisticated security systems and have no desire to learn.

But I'm lucky that my job allows me to live vicariously—if fictionally—through people who do.

Jade has been floating around my mind for a very long time—at least a decade. She was the first heroine I ever conceived, so having her story finally come to light has been very rewarding. And given her intensity, it seemed only right that she have a hero like the enigmatic Remy, who could challenge and intrigue her, and, eventually, be her true partner.

I hope you enjoy Jade and Remy's journey to finding love as much as I did. You can visit my Web site www.wendyetherington.com or contact me by regular mail at P.O. Box 3016, Irmo, SC 29063.

Take care and happy reading!

Wendy Etherington

A BREATH AWAY
Wendy Etherington

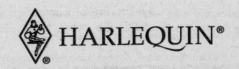

HARLEQUIN®

TORONTO • NEW YORK • LONDON
AMSTERDAM • PARIS • SYDNEY • HAMBURG
STOCKHOLM • ATHENS • TOKYO • MILAN • MADRID
PRAGUE • WARSAW • BUDAPEST • AUCKLAND

ISBN-13: 978-0-373-79314-3
ISBN-10: 0-373-79314-6

A BREATH AWAY

www.eHarlequin.com

Printed in U.S.A.

ABOUT THE AUTHOR

Though a voracious reader since childhood, Wendy Etherington spent much of her professional life in business and computer pursuits. Finally giving in to those creative impulses, she began writing romances. *A Breath Away* is her twelfth published novel and features a character she's spent a decade working to bring to life—a confident, kind-of-wounded, kick-ass chick named Jade.

Books by Wendy Etherington

HARLEQUIN BLAZE
263—JUST ONE TASTE...

HARLEQUIN TEMPTATION
944—PRIVATE LIES
958—ARE YOU LONESOME TONIGHT?
998—SPARKING HIS INTEREST
1027—THE ELEVENTH HOUR

HARLEQUIN FLIPSIDE
29—IF THE STILETTO FITS...

HARLEQUIN DUETS
76—MY PLACE OR YOURS?
93—CAN'T HELP FALLING IN LOVE
  HUNKA, HUNKA BURNIN' LOVE

To Kelly Adams, Linda Gabler and
Theresa Johnson, who took my kids to the movies
at a critical moment. You're neighbors I miss
and friends I cherish.

1

"WHERE'S MY PILE of money?"

Pissed off after an excruciatingly frustrating morning at the Atlanta airport, Jade Broussard glared at her cousin across his desk.

Rising from his black leather chair, Lucas grinned—the man was too charming for his own good. "Did I mention money?"

"A *pile*."

"Mmm. I suppose I did." He extended his arm toward one of the plush chairs in front of his desk. "You look exhausted. Coffee?"

Jade shook her head and instead prowled the room. His sleek yet posh office with its stunning view of Midtown was impressive. But then, she expected nothing less from Lucas. Everything he touched turned to gold, even though these days he was doing more pro bono work than litigating multi-million-dollar cases.

Instead of contemplating his attack of conscience, she recalled the phone conversation they'd had the night before.

"What do I have to do for this pile of money?"

"What you usually do—provide protection, investigate the crime."

"The police investigate crimes," she'd said, though he had her attention, a fact he no doubt realized.

"Just come. Please."

She'd come. What else could she do? He was the only family she had left.

"I'm not exhausted," she said finally.

"I should hope not. I sent a limo."

"I'm furious. Do you have any idea how crazy that airport is? Landing delays. Terminal changes. People ambling everywhere talking on cell phones. Security is a mess."

"They frisked you, didn't they?"

"They *tried.*"

As if he'd expected her travel woes, Lucas had the nerve to smirk.

"I'm walking through the airport, minding my own business, when some overly paranoid, jerk-face citizen spots my Beretta beneath my jacket. All hell breaks loose, people ducking, diving and screaming." She stalked toward him. "I'm a *professional.* I have a permit."

"Of course you do."

"I didn't draw the damn thing, you know."

"Though I imagine you were tempted."

She planted her hands on her hips, remembering—with renewed fury—the humiliation of being escorted to airport security. "You're damn right I was tempted. Freakin' terrorists. They're ruining this country."

"No doubt their goal. Perhaps if you'd waited until you got in the limo to retrieve your gun from your carry-on bag…"

She shrugged. "Yeah." She didn't feel whole without a side piece, though. She felt vulnerable. Exposed. Alone.

Shaking off the thread of irritation, she finally dropped into the chair in front of Lucas's desk and crossed her booted ankles. "What's this case about?" For double her usual fee, there had to be more to it than "provide protection, investigate the crime."

"A favor for a friend."

"What friend?"

"The friendly kind."

She smirked. "Cute. Where did you meet this friend?"

Lucas grinned, and his green eyes lit with an obviously favorable memory. "A bar. Yours, in fact."

"Beau's?"

"You own another bar?"

She frowned, ignoring the pang of grief that had never fully faded—even more than a decade after her parents' murders. Beau and Katy Broussard had been a staple of the bluesy French Quarter. Their deaths had completely changed the course of Jade's life. She'd inherited the bar, and eventually gotten vengeance on their killer, but she didn't have them— their laughter, their touch or their guidance. Revenge had been a hollow victory, just as she'd been warned it would be.

Normally she liked verbal sparring with her cousin, but if this case was somehow connected to her personally— through Beau's or her past—she didn't intend to waste time with chitchat.

"Who's the friend, Lucas?" she asked, her tone hard.

"Remington Tremaine."

Jade fought a flinch, but apparently didn't quite pull it off, since Lucas nodded.

"He said you'd know him."

Her mouth had gone dry, but she forced herself to think fast. Tremaine was not someone she wanted anywhere near her cousin. Dangerous didn't even begin to describe the man. "How long ago did you meet him?"

"Three years ago. We bonded over a glass or two of Southern Comfort, and he's been a client ever since. His family has old San Francisco money, mostly from real estate and vineyards, but Remy loves art."

No doubt stolen.

"I've arranged for the sale of some beautiful and rare pieces over the past few years," Lucas continued.

While Lucas watched closely for her reaction, Jade simply nodded. Though she knew her cousin had a not-so-stellar past with the law, he'd long ago gone straight. These sales were legit.

Of course they are. Who'd suspect a genteel, handsome-as-sin art collector of anything more serious than spending more on wine than a car?

And wasn't that precisely the point?

"What happened to Tremaine?" she asked.

"He was shot outside a restaurant here in Midtown two nights ago."

A thousand thoughts rushed her brain instantly, and she fought to find one question she could ask. "How bad?"

"The bullet grazed his arm. He's fine."

"Which restaurant?"

"Plush."

Jade finally managed to shake off the shock of hearing Tremaine's name. "Plush?"

"A happening place for the idle rich and semifamous."

"Naturally." The bastard would fit right in.

"You'll be able to see for yourself. The whole thing is on videotape."

Jade raised her eyebrows. "You have a videotape of the shooting?"

"The police do."

"And how did you find that out?"

"Not from the cops. The restaurant manager told Remy."

"Convenient. What about press coverage?"

"Light. Unfortunately, a shooting isn't big news in Atlanta unless somebody famous is involved. This particular restaurant insisted the cops keep everything quiet and had the pull to make it happen. 'A local diner was shot last night' was as much as the media got."

Something positive in this mess, and yet the most important question was as yet unanswered. They might as well get to it. "Who suggested hiring me—you or him?"

"You know him from…before, don't you?"

Jade shook her head. Her past was something Lucas knew she didn't—*couldn't*—discuss.

Eyeing her, he stroked his chin. "He asked me to hire you. He called from the hospital emergency room, in fact."

"You're that close?"

"No."

Her cousin was a smart man. Brilliant, in fact. He'd sensed way more than was wise for him. He had a nice life and a beautiful new wife. He didn't need the complications Tremaine had laid at his doorstep.

Some friend.

"He's not really an art dealer, is he?" Lucas asked into the charged silence.

No. No, he certainly wasn't.

Remington Tremaine was many things—arrogant and bold high among them. He was sneaky and obsessively private. He flouted rules and codes, and seemed to operate by a morality that made no sense to anyone but him. He was obscenely handsome and knew it. He was a dark mystery, the kind that inspired feminine sighs of longing and male snorts of envy. The kind whispered about by the very few who knew his true history.

The two most important things Jade knew about him, however, were the two things she absolutely couldn't share with Lucas. One, Remington Tremaine was a former international art and jewel thief. And two, he currently was an undercover agent with the National Security Agency.

In this day of dedicated searches for terrorists, some of the "softer" crimes went unnoticed. Thieves were pushed aside in favor of tracking whispers about major terrorist attacks. But a small portion of NSA bosses suspected the spoils of certain burglaries were being funneled into terrorist groups, so there was still a group of agents who focused their talents on investigating that connection. Tremaine was part of that group, and the one most speculated about.

None of the other agents knew how the NSA had lured him away from his cushy life of crime to the side of law and order, but he'd apparently done enough to keep the directors from prosecuting him for his previous transgressions. She'd always thought he was one of those forgive-you-to-get-the-bigger-bad-guy deals that were made with criminals all the time.

What the hell had the NSA been thinking giving him a cover as an art dealer? That was like giving the drunk the keys to the bar.

"Dammit, Jade," Lucas said as he stood, "I have a right to know what's going on."

Bracing her hands against the wooden arms of her chair, Jade rose slowly. At only thirty-three, she suddenly felt old and tired. But she was also furious. How dare Tremaine bring the NSA and God only knew what kind of criminals from his past to her doorstep? To Lucas's doorstep—his supposed friend?

The past never really leaves us, her business partner and mentor, Frank Williams, had once said. How right he was.

"No, you don't have a right," she said, her gaze burning into his. "As of now, this is *my* problem. I want you to go back to work, back to helping people who actually need it. I want you to forget about Remington Tremaine. If anybody asks, you arranged the sale of some artwork for him, and that's it. You know nothing else. Got it?"

Green eyes so like her own flashed back at her. "I won't sit by and let you do this by yourself."

Though she appreciated his blind support, she didn't soften her gaze. "Where is he?"

"Someplace safe."

"Dammit, Lucas, I don't have time for games." She leaned over his desk. *"Where is he?"*

"You're not cutting me out."

"Oh, yes, I am."

"Then I have no idea where he is." He turned his back on her.

She'd kill Tremaine for this, for involving her family in their sordid world of intrigue. Whoever was after him didn't need to worry. She'd eliminate the problem and relish the act. Mr. Tremaine should look up her records. After reading the file about what had happened to the last idiot who'd messed with her family, he'd undoubtedly change his mind about getting to her through Lucas.

She hated herself for scaring her cousin, but she did it anyway. Lucas had no training and belonged nowhere near the danger surrounding Tremaine. "What about Vanessa?" she whispered to Lucas's back.

Predictably, he spun to face her. He didn't look so confident anymore.

This is what you do, girl. Find a weakness. Exploit it. Get the mission done.

"What about her?" he asked, his gaze hard and furious. And anxious.

"Your wife isn't part of this."

"Of course not."

"But she will be if you persist."

Lucas's hands fisted at his sides. "Are you threatening me?"

"No." She walked around his desk and stopped just inches from him. She looked up into his handsome, trusted, beloved face. "But *they* will."

"Who?"

Whatever scum from her old life that seemed determined to follow her into this one. Why had Tremaine contacted her? If he'd been shot on the job, why hadn't he gone to the NSA? Had his cover been blown? Had he lost faith in the agency?

Or was this shooting personal? Was that why he'd involved Lucas? To scare or intimidate her into taking his case?

Once upon a time she'd been an NSA agent, as well, so she could understand the disastrous implications of any of those scenarios. But she'd retired—and not on the best of terms. Even though she now owned a security and investigations company, and could protect the average John Q. Citizen, she didn't have the power or contacts of the agency.

So why did Tremaine want her?

"Who would threaten me?" Lucas asked, bringing her thoughts back to him.

In disgust, she knew the vow of secrecy to her government only expired on her death, and no matter how bitterly she and the agency had parted, she owed them her silence about their ways and their world. She trusted Lucas, but she couldn't share this with him.

"Whomever shot Tremaine." She laid her hands on his shoulders. "This is outside your realm, Lucas. Admit it and let me deal with it."

He shrugged off her touch.

She fought against the hurt of his rejection. "Where is he?"

"Gone."

Whatever she'd expected, it wasn't that. She goggled at him. *"Gone?"*

"No one knows he left. They think he's holed up in his hotel room."

"They?"

"Everybody but me—including the police."

Resisting the urge to pull her hair out by the roots—she'd save that bit of torture for Tremaine—she paced the room.

Damn the arrogant man. He should have let the NSA take him underground until the whole mess could be sorted out. Yet she knew, and not just because he'd called Lucas, that he'd abandoned protocol and forged his own plan. He'd no doubt continue to do so.

Lucas blocked her path. "Dammit, Jade, I want to help."

She stepped back. "You can't." She wouldn't let him. Risking the highly trained people in her own agency was going to be hard enough. "Where is he, Lucas?"

His eyes cold, he bit out his response. "He has a room at the Marriott Marquis. He said he'd meet you there later."

As he turned away, she resisted slugging him and knocking some sense into his hard head. She loved him like a brother, and surely he'd get over his snit fit eventually.

He was her one connection to family. And yet, for her job, she'd hurt him.

Just another day in paradise.

USING THE KEY to Tremaine's posh, two-bedroom hotel suite Lucas had given her, Jade took advantage of the solitude to snoop and make phone calls.

She noted the neutral black, bone and tan colors, as well as the glass, leather and steel that made up the contemporary decor and wondered if it suited Tremaine. The sumptuous living and dining area was as large as most people's apartments, and there was a fully stocked bar. She could certainly understand why he preferred the suite to whatever holding room the NSA would stuff him in until they were ready to launch the complicated investigation into an undercover agent's shooting.

But why had he gone against protocol to hire *her?*

She was good, and her team was great, but even with her and her partner's network of contacts, they couldn't get inside current NSA files. She and Tremaine had never met and knew each other only by reputation. Why was he hiring—and essentially trusting—her instead of moving under the NSA's protective umbrella?

The answer seemed too simple to be correct—he didn't trust the NSA.

Smart man.

Whatever his reasoning, he'd cleverly hooked her. She didn't like violence coming anywhere near Lucas, and if protecting Tremaine meant protecting her cousin, she'd bite her tongue and do it. Plus, despite her urge to scoff at the pretty boy's troubles, she was reluctantly intrigued about the legendary thief.

So, it seemed she and Tremaine were stuck with each other. She doubted they would get along—she'd heard too much about his tendency to follow only the rules that were convenient for him. In her mind, rules existed for a good reason—convenient or not.

His light-fingered past didn't win him any points with her, either. Even if he'd been a very good thief.

Could you use *good* and *light-fingered* in the same sentence without sounding ridiculous?

Not in her book.

She used her cell phone to call her partner, Frank, and her best guards to her side. They'd all be on planes in the morning. She didn't see any point in their coming sooner, since their client was MIA, and she preferred facing him alone at the moment.

If she decided to kill him, she could always bury his body and not involve her business in the crime.

Snooping-wise, she got very little that she didn't already know. He'd left his luggage—purposefully, she was sure—so she found shaving cream, shampoo, condoms and a spicy, exotic cologne that would no doubt suit him. His wardrobe consisted of custom-made suits in charcoal and black and Italian loafers with tassels.

Art magazines and a highbrow novel encompassed his printed collection. And though she took great delight in gliding a razor blade down all the seams of his expensive leather bags to check for hidden compartments, she found nothing of interest.

If he was arrogant, at least he wasn't stupid.

At dinnertime, she sampled from the fruit basket on the coffee table. Late into the night, she flipped around the TV channels and found nothing that could hold her interest for more than a moment or two.

Nearly all her clients begged for her services. She'd worked for rock stars needing protection from overzealous fans, wealthy businessmen who wanted to protect their assets from thieves. Even politicians, who always seemed dogged by threats and stalkers, called her and her team every election year.

They all did what she said without question, either out of fear for themselves or their families. They relied on her expertise.

No one had ever been so cocky as to order her services through a third party, then not even bother to show up for his purchase. She was sure the contrast wasn't lost on Tremaine.

At l:00 a.m., she locked the guest-bedroom door, showered, re-dressed, then lay on top of the bed. She might as well get some rest if her client was going to continue to ignore her.

In a fitful sleep, she dreamed about her parents. They stood behind their ancient walnut bar at Beau's, their arms crossed over their chests, their faces set with disappointment. Guilt washed over her. She wanted to tell them she hadn't failed them. She wanted to explain she was sorry she hadn't been there to protect them....

Then she was hugging Lucas. She lay her head against his chest and delighted in the beat of his heart, realizing there was still one person in the world who loved her unconditionally, who shared her blood. She relaxed, letting the feeling of security wash through her.

His lips whispered over her cheek. "I need your help," he said softly.

In less than a second, she realized she was no longer dreaming. There were indeed lips against her cheek. Warm, soft, persuasive lips attached to a warm, hard, male body. Neither of which belonged to her cousin.

Though training and instincts screamed danger, she paused

to breathe in the scent of a spicy, exotic cologne and a faint smell of whiskey and realized the rumors about her new client must be true.

He was very good with his hands.

By the moonlight streaming through the window, she could see he lay on his side, pressed against her, his lips sending shivers of delight skating down her spine, his clever fingers gliding up her stomach. Under her shirt. That simple touch ignited sensual sparks inside her, creating a longing she fought to ignore.

Did he intend to disarm her before seducing her? Somehow, she doubted he'd bother.

"Move your hand up another inch, Tremaine, and you'll lose it."

With a quick flip, she'd straddled him and pressed her Beretta to the center of his forehead.

The rogue had the nerve to smile. "My, my, Ms. Broussard. Is this how you greet all your clients?"

"Only the ones who pick the lock to my bedroom."

"You could hardly call that thing on the door a lock."

No doubt she could have gotten past it herself, but what infuriated her was that she hadn't heard him. He'd come through the outer door, crossed the living room, opened the bedroom door, crossed that room, then *slid into bed with her* before she'd been aware. Normally, she'd have heard him when he put the key card in the exterior door lock. Either she was really tired, or he was even more skilled than she'd imagined.

She also wasn't crazy about the way she'd responded to his touch. For a moment she'd relished the contact with him and wanted more. Staring down into his sculpted face, his silvery eyes glittering back at her, his jet-black hair gleaming almost blue in the low light, she wanted him still. His innate sensuality was even more potent in person than in pictures, though some part of her managed to recognize that an attraction to her client was a weakness she couldn't afford.

More aggravated at herself than him, she holstered her pistol. "Is there a particular reason you're in bed with me?"

"It's my bed."

"It's the wrong bed. This is the guest room."

He grinned. "My mistake."

"I'm sure. Where the hell have you been?"

"On an errand of mercy."

She rolled her eyes.

"Pictures don't do you justice, Agent Broussard."

"That's *former* Agent Broussard, and I'll have to return the compliment." Her body still hummed from the feel of his fingers. Men—especially male clients—didn't overwhelm her. They didn't affect her personally.

He braced his hands at her waist. "We could continue what we started."

To her surprise, Jade was tempted. She held nearly everyone at a distance, so she rarely took the time to indulge in sex. She was definitely aware of the hard ridge of male flesh pressed intimately between her legs. She already knew his hands promised magic.

Their physical attraction was as obvious in the room as the bed they were lying on. Her stomach fluttered with need. Her fingers tingled. All she had to do was lean down, press her lips to his…

"Bad idea," she said, jerking back.

As she climbed off him, his eyes darkened with seemingly genuine regret. "Perhaps another time."

She didn't comment and glanced at the clock on the

bedside table: 4:00 a.m. It was time to get back to business. "You want to tell me who shot you and why?"

"If I knew that, I wouldn't need you, would I?"

"Why *do* you need me? Why don't you trot back to Washington and let the NSA deal with this?"

He rolled off the bed and gained his feet with a grace that she was certain had gotten him through more than one second-story window undetected and unscathed. "I'll tell you everything over coffee."

Somehow I doubt that.

Watching him stride from the room, Jade's gaze slid down his lean body, covered in tailored black pants and a black ribbed turtleneck, and wondered if he'd really given up his former profession.

How many people had he made a fool of in his murky past? How many beds had he crawled into? Was his present just as devious? She knew that less than half of the rumors about her were accurate. Was it the same for him? What was his real story?

He intrigued her more than was wise. In her line of work, she had to maintain a professional distance in order to serve her clients well. In her private life, space was just as welcome. But the moments of personal intimacy she'd just shared with Tremaine already had her thinking of him as something more than a client, and she couldn't quite shake the lingering tremors of desire.

Not good. Not good at all.

Was she really crazy enough to help him?

Apparently, since she sighed and stalked after him.

She did, however, double-check to be sure her ammunition clip was fully loaded first.

2

REMY EYED JADE "The Arrow" Broussard over the rim of his coffee mug and again marveled that the hard, determined woman now pacing in front of him had been melting in his arms only moments earlier, her fiery hair tangled around his fingers, her voice husky with sleep.

He wondered if she knew as much about him as he did about her. He wondered if her nickname was well-earned. Because of her deadly sharp shooting skills and her tendency to be a rule-follower—at least by the slippery NSA standards—he'd been as surprised as anybody when she'd suddenly resigned two years ago to follow her partner, Frank Williams, into the private sector. Remy reflected on the way she'd leaned into his touch. She'd relaxed quite a bit since leaving government work.

A handy convenience for him.

"I don't appreciate you dragging my cousin into this," she said when she finally stopped pacing, planting her hands on her hips and glaring at him.

"I needed protection. I asked a trusted advisor for guidance."

"One who just happens to be my cousin. You had to know."

He'd known. His friendship with Lucas had just been a happy by-product of his deep-seated need to find out more about the lady currently scowling at him.

In fact, he could admit—at least to himself—that he had a miniobsession when it came to Jade Broussard. Ever since he'd seen the first NSA case file involving her, he'd researched her, wondered about her and even sought out her cousin in the hopes of someday meeting her.

After last night's shooting, she seemed the obvious choice to help him solve a lifelong mystery. She'd single-mindedly gotten revenge for her family. Maybe she could do the same for him.

"I certainly check out all my advisors before taking them on," he said finally.

"Do you ever give anybody a straight answer?"

He smiled faintly. "Not if I can help it." Just for the thrill, he let his gaze slide down her body, which was surprisingly curvy for such a fierce and serious woman. "Surely, it's the same for you."

"Very few people ask me questions," she said.

"Too intimidated?"

"I imagine."

"You'll have a hard time affecting me the same way, Jade."

Her shoulders jerked at his use of her first name. She clearly didn't like the intimacy. She liked their attraction even less.

Ironically, he relished her presence.

After talking himself out of contacting her for so long— deciding she wouldn't want anything to do with a former thief—having her close was an interesting kind of torture.

She would never understand what had driven him to his former life. Yet, despite the philosophical distance between them, his blood sizzled hotter every minute they were together. He had to curl his hands into fists to keep from reaching for her.

He'd snuck into her bed to rattle her, to see if the effect she had on him from a distance would strengthen when they touched. But even he hadn't anticipated being knocked so far off balance. He hadn't expected the temptation to be so strong.

"I want some answers from you, Tremaine," she said as she resumed pacing. "I want them now and I want them straight, or I'm dumping you and going back home."

"No compassion for an old colleague?"

"No."

"I was shot, you know."

"Whoopee. Been there myself a few times."

Though he'd known this, he raised his eyebrows. "Who got the jump on *you?*"

"An electronics thief who wanted to turn Miami Beach into his own personal illegal superstore for assorted bad guys. Still have the scar on my upper thigh."

That would have been Romildo Ramirez. "And how did he make out?"

Her gaze raked him. "Not as well as you obviously did."

"Just a scratch for me, I'll admit. But still a rather rude end to a lovely dinner."

"Who'd want to shoot you over dinner?"

"That's what I want you to find out."

"Dinner with whom? About what?"

All business, this one. Something else he'd known—a quality that was good for his case, though maybe not for his libido. "Is there any chance of you calling me Remy?"

Her vivid green eyes flashed. "No."

"We're going to be pretty…intimate over the next couple of weeks."

"We're going to be close professionally. Close and intimate are two different things. Dinner—who and what?"

She didn't trust him at all. Smart woman. "I was having

dinner with a female friend. A *personal* female friend," he clarified, though he was sure she'd figured that already. "She enjoys my taste in wine and new restaurants. My interest in art, frankly, baffles her, but then we don't often go into deep discussions about light and symmetry."

Jade smirked. "I'm sure."

"She's a charming companion when I'm between buying trips. Or, for our purposes, between *cases*."

"Which you are now?"

"For the most part. I'd just started on some research for a new project."

"So this shooting is personal?"

"I think so."

She stopped, glancing at him. "Related to your past."

"Yes."

"Who?"

"I have several people in mind."

Her eyes flashed with anger. "Thieves?"

She would never understand his past. He resisted the urge to sigh. He knew this, after all. "They all have illegal connections."

"Have any of them threatened you? Do any of them know what you do now?"

"My cover is secure, and getting shot is pretty threatening." Holding up the videotape he'd procured a few hours ago, he crossed the room to the VCR and popped the cassette in. "Maybe this will help."

"The tape of the shooting? Lucas said you—" She stopped as he walked back toward her.

She glared up at him, and he could tell she didn't like his proximity or their size difference. He was a solid six-two, whereas she was only five-seven.

"How did you get the tape?" she asked.

He returned to his seat on the sofa, leaning against the cushions and laying one arm along the back. His effort at casualness was deliberate, since he felt anything but. Both the shooting and the woman who stood so close had knocked him dangerously askew. "From the police."

"They just handed over a copy?"

"Not exactly."

She looked disgusted. "If we're going to do this, you can't just swipe anything you want."

"Why not?" he asked reasonably, though when she opened her mouth to no doubt tell him why, he continued, "I made a copy and returned the original."

"Is that where you've been the last twelve hours?"

"How do you know I've been gone twelve hours?"

"'Cause I've been here nearly that long." She dropped onto the opposite end of the sofa and propped her feet—encased in dark green alligator boots—on the coffee table.

"I only spent a small part of that time at the police station. Their security is shockingly lax."

"I bet you say that about everyone."

"True."

Anxious to view the tape himself, Remy pressed the play button on the remote. The digital timer in the upper right-hand corner allowed him to fast-forward to the moment he was interested in, though later he'd watch the hour before the shooting to look for any details that might be relevant.

At 7:52 p.m., a white male with dark-brown hair, about five-ten in height and dressed in a waiter's uniform, walked out of the French doors to Remy's right. Holding a bread basket to conceal his gun, he headed straight to Remy's table, but at about five feet from his target, another waiter crossed his path, bumping into him and knocking the basket to the floor. The other waiter knelt to clean up the mess as the shooter directed his attention to Remy. Then, in either a panic or a rage, he fired off two shots.

Remy yanked his date under the table as the shooter leaped over the low brick wall surrounding the patio and disappeared from view.

He remembered well his heart hammering, his arm burning and his thoughts racing. He'd tried to block out the panicked shouts and cries as he palmed the .22 pistol he carried concealed in an ankle holster, quickly returning the weapon to its hiding place when he realized no more shots were coming. The waiter who'd knocked into the shooter had crawled beneath the table to check on them, and Remy had the presence of mind and training to morph into a shocked and outraged art executive as the police were called and he and his date were sent to the hospital.

Jade asked for the remote, and he handed it to her without comment. She ran the tape back three times before asking, "Do you make a habit of eating at this restaurant?"

"I've never been there, though I did make a reservation two days before."

"Do you often sit outside at restaurants?"

"Hardly ever in February. But there was a live band, a number of heaters, and my companion pleaded."

"You don't know the shooter I take it."

"Never seen him before, and the tape is pretty grainy. We can try running his image through the usual channels, though."

"Let the police chase that. He doesn't seem like a professional."

Remy agreed—and all the more reason the shooting didn't make sense. "Rather lousy aim."

"And the whole plan was bad. Too risky, too public." She angled her head. "Unless the intent was simply a warning."

He nodded. He'd considered that, as well. In fact, given his suspect short list, it was likely.

"Who would hire such an incompetent idiot?"

"Somebody desperate, equally stupid or very, very clever." She glanced at him for the first time since the tape started. "I'd feel better if it had been a good hit."

He was nearly sure she didn't mean a *successful* attempt on his life. Still, he agreed. The clumsiness of the whole business was somehow more chilling. It was out of place and unfamiliar in their world.

The intrigue and danger they lived with day-to-day made them suspicious of everyone, unable to trust, and forced them to distance themselves from most people. As a result, they were paranoid. And very careful.

But he'd made mistakes in his past. He'd already paid for some and there was one whose bill seemed to finally be due.

"I need everything you have on your date and the people you believe are behind the shooting."

"Got it." He reached beneath his shirt and pulled out a minidisk, then handed it to her. He was interested in what she'd come up with. More than him? Or at least something different? He was nearly positive who was responsible, but he needed to be sure before he risked revealing details about his past to Jade and her team. "My date's clean, though."

She glanced at the disk before setting it on the table in front of them. "Part of your mercy mission?"

"I had to stash her somewhere until I can figure out what's going on."

"Where?"

"Puerto Rico—a lovely resort and spa."

"How'd you get her there?"

"My LearJet."

"You have a private plane?"

He liked the way her eyes turned hot when she was annoyed. He wondered what they looked like when she was aroused. "Mmm. It's handy."

"Bought on your government salary?"

"Certainly not."

"I don't want to hear about it."

Though his heart pounded, he watched her with the appearance of calm. The Arrow probably never stepped outside the lines. "Perhaps I bought it with my ill-gotten gains. Maybe everything I have is tainted with greed and deception."

Her gaze slid back to his. "Maybe it is."

"I'm a legitimate art dealer."

"I'm sure you are."

"I need your help, not your judgment. I can't share my past with the police, and I'm not telling the NSA any more than they already know." He rose to pour more coffee. "Are you taking my case or not?" He thought he'd assured himself of her participation by going through Lucas, but maybe he'd been wrong about their bond.

"I'm going to have to dig deeply into your past."

"I know."

"You'll have to give me names, dates, places."

"The disk contains plenty."

"I also want your impressions of people. Not just a scroll of data."

He nodded.

"I'm taking your case."

"Thank you."

He was going to have to share things he'd rather not. He was going to have to relive times better left buried. He might even have to trust Jade Broussard.

She didn't respect him, and obviously abhorred his illegal past. He especially didn't want to face her judgment, because then he might have to admit that in the black-and-white of the world, he'd spent most of his life in the dark.

JADE KNEW the idea of sharing didn't sit well with her client. Well, at least they had that in common.

Very little else, but they had that.

"Let's start with the present. You're sure the shooting isn't job-related?"

"That's the most logical conclusion."

Again, she noted the careful choice of words. He didn't exactly agree, didn't answer her question, but he didn't disagree, either. He kept the flow of conversation going without revealing his thoughts. She'd bet it served him well—in both legal and illegal situations.

"Have you talked to Hillman?" she asked, expecting him to say he hadn't.

When Tremaine nodded, she suppressed her surprise and asked, "What did he say?"

"What you'd expect—come in from the field, we'll protect you."

"And you said *no?*" She was trying to picture *anybody*—

even the man next to her—disobeying a direct order from Jordan Hillman, a high-level director at the NSA, who oversaw every active undercover operation and was one of the most secretly powerful men in the country.

"I said nothing."

"Naturally. You're good at that."

"It comes in handy at times." He slid his hand along the back of the leather sofa they shared. The move was a sinuous caress, one that made her blood hum even as part of her remained professional, observing how well he fit into the contemporary decor of the room, though she was sure he'd look equally at home among oxblood club chairs and gas lanterns.

He was a dichotomy.

A mystery she longed to unfold. Much to her frustration.

"So, he thinks you're coming in?" she asked in an effort to force her brain to concentrate fully on her job.

"I imagine he's figured out by now that I'm not."

Great. Talk about a war on multiple fronts. "So we have them after you, too?"

"No. I'll call him and tell him I think I have a handle on who's responsible."

"He'll expect a full report—names, motives, etcetera."

"Not from me."

What was he holding back? She had little doubt he was only *pretending* to cooperate. He had an agenda here that went beyond the botched shooting.

As she was mulling over the possibilities—maybe the shooting *was* NSA related, and he and Hillman were trying to draw her back into the agency—he reached out and stroked her jaw.

She jerked back.

"I wondered if you'd be hard and rough," he said, seeming unaffected by her retreat. "You're not. Somehow, you still have compassion and tenderness. I wonder how twelve years at the NSA didn't stamp it out of you."

She was surprised to realize her throat was dry, and her face was warm where he'd touched her. "How do you know I put in twelve years?"

"I know a lot about you, Jade Katherine Broussard."

His silver eyes turned to the color of smoke, and the heat emanating from his body slid around her like a cashmere wrap. There had been times in her life when her spirit had been so cold and lonely she'd have given anything for that sensation.

But she'd found strength and purpose in her work. She had loyal friends and colleagues and didn't need anyone to hold her hand when she ran into trouble.

There were times, though, when she longed for something more. For a relationship like the one her parents had shared. For someone who both understood and challenged her. For white-hot passion that overwhelmed her, burning down the walls she'd so carefully built.

"You're very beautiful," he said, leaning toward her.

She blinked. What had she been *thinking?* Had she actually been *daydreaming* in the middle of an interrogation? The man was a client, an admitted thief and probably a master manipulator.

She ignored his compliment—which was no doubt empty, anyway. "When did you last talk to Hillman?"

"I called him last night."

The chief guy took his call? Another oddity in an already strange case. "You didn't detour to Washington on your way to Puerto Rico?"

"No."

She planted her boots on the floor and sat forward, her forearms resting on her thighs. "You talked to *him?* Not his assistant?"

"Yes."

"Yet you said you were *pretty much* between cases. *Just doing a little research.* If you're consulting with the top man, you're doing a great deal more than that."

He said nothing for several moments, then he smiled. "Perhaps I am."

"That's it?" She stayed in her seat and held her temper by the barest margin. "Look, I've had about enough of your evasive answers. And your mysterious past doesn't intrigue me, it annoys me. If we're going to make this…"

"Relationship?"

"…unconventional partnership work, you've got to trust me."

Still smiling, he shook his head. "Isn't gonna happen."

He trusted no one. She understood, since she felt exactly the same way.

"But—just so you know—there isn't a big case or mystery," he added. "I always work directly with Hillman. That was part of my agreement when I signed on with the NSA."

She got over her irritation long enough to be impressed. "Convenient."

He shrugged. "Mostly it was a power thing." Grinning, he added, "I like having it all on my side."

The guy wasn't just slippery good, he was amazing good. He charmed and disarmed, even as he stole your wallet. He worked for the government and still made a profit. "I imagine you do."

She stood to pace, as she often did when she was thinking. But tonight she did so because she couldn't think. He was distracting. His smile, his sleek good looks, his craftiness, even his evasiveness. She'd lied when she'd said his mysterious past didn't intrigue her.

In truth, she wanted to know more. She wanted to know all. And more than the professional details. Her body wanted *intimate* details.

But her job required her to set aside her curiosity and pretend her senses weren't completely overwhelmed by the temptation he presented. "Why don't you want Hillman to know the shooting is part of your past?"

"I don't trust him to keep his word and leave my past in the grave where I buried it."

She didn't trust Hillman, either, so her opinion of her client rose a bit. She also respected his intentions to move ahead, away from the criminal life he'd led.

But she knew she had to hold her sympathy in check. She was intrigued by him, her body wanted him, but she wasn't sure she really *liked* him.

She'd solve his case, take his money and protect her cousin. As long as she kept those distinct objectives in mind, they'd all come out just fine.

"But I'd think you and Hillman would be buddies," she said, not trying to hide her sarcasm. "Of the same mind and all. You're the poster boy for trying any means necessary to get the bigger, badder criminal of the moment, after all."

"Yes, I imagine that's his philosophy. I guess you don't agree."

She crossed her arms over her chest and scowled at him. "You guess correctly."

"You don't think the government should make deals with the other side?"

Well aware he was asking her if she agreed with Hillman's

decision to offer a deal to him in particular, she refused to soften her stance. "No, I don't."

"Leopards don't change their spots."

"Not in my experience."

He simply nodded.

During her NSA career, she'd been appalled by some of the arrangements made with midlevel criminals in order to bring down their bosses. The idea that justice was negotiated in a boardroom, and that any wrongdoing could be wiped out by ratting out somebody else, was abhorrent to her.

Tremaine had benefited from such an agreement, which she'd always resented. What had precipitated his change of sides? And why had he taken the government's deal in the first place?

To save his own hide, most likely, though he did nothing now to defend himself. What was up with him? And why did she have to be so damn interested in digging beneath the surface?

"So, that's the present—at least professionally. But we haven't talked about the *personal* present. Friends and lovers." She watched his expression, hoping he'd squirm. "Anybody there have it in for you?"

"Like if I slept with my best friend's wife?"

Given his lothario reputation, she certainly wouldn't be surprised, but somehow she didn't see the man before her putting himself in that position. He'd be selective about his bed partners, and he'd consider all the options and consequences before taking that step.

What else about him had been exaggerated?

"Yeah, like that," she said finally.

"I don't have a best friend, so no."

Her pulse jumped. How did he manage to get to her that

way? She cleared her throat. "So now that we've covered the present, it's time for the past."

She could have sworn she saw him flinch, but he recovered quickly.

"Of course," he said, smiling with the easy charm that seemed as natural to him as breathing. "But before we do, I think it's important that we explore our unexpected connection."

"What unexpected connection?"

"The fact that I'd much rather get you in bed than investigate my own shooting." As she ground to a halt, he raised his eyebrows, looking inviting as sin. "I assume the sentiment is returned?"

3

JADE FOUGHT TO ignore her rapid heartbeat. She forced herself to drag clean air into her lungs, to expel it and to calm her erotic thoughts.

She failed miserably.

Instead, she imagined her client's body beneath her, his erection pressed against the pulsing need between her legs.

They'd been that close a short time ago, but now she envisioned their clothes disappearing. His body would be hard and sleek. Ripples of need and heat would surge through her. His hands would pleasure her beyond her wildest dreams. She'd satisfy an itch she didn't even know she had until she'd met him.

"It hardly matters if we want each other," she said, humiliated to find herself breathless. "We're both professionals, so we're not going to do anything about it."

He smiled, his gaze locking with hers. "Aren't we?"

As he rose and started toward her, she froze. She ordered her feet to move, but they didn't. The look in his eyes needed no explanation as to his intent, and though the professional remained lurking inside her—the one *usually* front and center—the desire rolling through her body was overwhelming her instincts.

When he stopped in front of her, he cupped her cheek in his hand and angled her face toward him. "If you're going to shoot, shoot to kill, because I'm not backing away."

Then his lips were on hers, persuasive and demanding, but still soft. Her heartbeat accelerated as he slid his tongue inside her mouth, drawing her more deeply beneath his spell, causing the final vestiges of restraint to fall away.

She pressed her body against his, molding herself to the hard planes of his chest, his hardened penis against her stomach. Desire pooled between her legs.

Inhaling the scent of his expensive cologne, she let him lead her to hunger and need, to fan the flames of their attraction and send the temperature from simmering to red-hot.

He was a virtual stranger, not to mention a client, and she watched herself from a distance, not really believing she was touching him and letting him touch her in return. She felt energized in his arms. And exhilarated. And safe.

It was the thought of safety that brought reality crashing back.

She was supposed to be protecting *him*. She was supposed to solve his case, help him get his life back under control, then send him on his way.

She wrenched herself out of his arms. Breathing hard, she held out her hand. "We can't do this."

He grabbed her hand and jerked her against him. "I sure as hell don't see any reasons not to."

"Sure you do. You're just ignoring them."

"Sex releases tension."

"Sex complicates."

"You don't like complications?"

"No, and I don't have sex with clients."

"Is that a hard and fast rule, or just a guideline?"

She braced her feet apart and glared at him. "Don't make me prove I can take you down anytime I want to, Tremaine."

"Back to last names, are we? Maybe I should prove how quickly I can have you moaning—even screaming—my name."

"Dream on."

"How about I demonstrate instead?"

Bang, bang, bang.

They jumped apart and darted toward the door.

"Room service!" came the cry from the hall.

Jade had her Beretta in her hand as she positioned herself against the wall next to the door. "You order anything?"

"No."

Her client had drawn a small pistol—from his ankle holster, no doubt—and took his place behind her. "Surely I'm not being stalked by someone with bad aim *and* a complete absence of originality. *Room service,*" he added in disgust.

Jade silently agreed, though she was pretty sure she recognized their *waiter's* voice. She peered through the peephole and did, indeed, see David Washington and Mo Leger. They waved.

Stifling an eye roll, she said, "They're mine," then holstered her weapon and opened the door.

"Hey, boss," David said, saluting. Tan, handsome and lean, his six-foot-six body was way too long for the waiter's uniform he wore.

Mo—every bit as tall, plus considerably heavier and darker—pushed a white-tablecloth-covered cart into the suite. He'd opted for a maintenance man's gray jumpsuit. "You might wanna hold back lookin' through the peephole, Chief. We coulda blasted you."

"I recognized your voice," Jade said with a trace of annoyance. Because of their sense of timing? She didn't want to go there.

She supposed it was too much to expect these two to stop treating their cases like elaborate games. But of course, to men like David and Mo—and probably Remington Tremaine, as well—chasing the bad guys was a game. One they played with deadly seriousness at times, but one they still found humor and enjoyment in.

She wished she could say she still had fun. Somewhere she'd lost the fire and passion, though she never considered doing anything else. It was all she knew and all she had.

After she made introductions among the men, David asked Tremaine, "So, you're NSA?"

When Tremaine hesitated to confirm, Jade said, "If you want our help, my people have to have information. I told them what was in your dossier."

"What little you have?"

"Keep it up, Mr. Fancy-art-dealer, and I'll find your would-be assassin just so I can swear my allegiance to him."

Mo and David gave her strange looks—she couldn't recall a time they'd seen her banter with a client—so before their curiosity got the best of them, she said, "His trouble isn't about a case. It's about his *former* profession."

Hell, she'd kissed the man and guilt—or attraction or weakness—already had her glossing over the fact that he used to take other people's stuff for a living.

"Sit down, and I'll fill you in," she added.

"Over breakfast," David said.

Jade glanced at the cart. "You brought food?"

Mo and David exchanged smiles. "Among other things."

OTHER THINGS turned out to be computers, surveillance equipment and instruments Remy couldn't begin to identify.

He was only marginally competent with computers, but he certainly recognized the weapons, ammunition clips, binoculars and communications devices—including headsets, microphones, cameras and bugs. But there were also black boxes that lit up or emitted a series of beeps, a control that looked suspiciously like a detonator and handheld wands that might be lasers.

If somebody had told him he was going to learn to swing a light saber, he wouldn't have been surprised in the least.

While he used technology to his advantage on occasion, his strength was his ability to get personal, to read body language, to discern the significance of expressions and reactions. He liked touching things and people. Reading an electronic gauge or tracking some blip on a radar screen held no appeal for him.

Mo, however, was clearly in his element. As he checked out the information on the disk Remy had provided, his walnut-colored hands commanded a laptop keyboard the way the best teenage techno-geek could only dream of doing. Since he was extremely fierce-looking, the thought of him as a geek made Remy smile.

Remy's amusement faded when his gaze slid to Jade, leaning over David's shoulder as she pointed to one of the mysterious black boxes on the dining room table. His attraction—correction, his overwhelming *need*—was interfering with the case. As much as he'd looked forward to finally meeting her, he hadn't anticipated that complication.

This case was about his *life*. And while there were many people who couldn't care less, he certainly placed a high value on his own skin.

But when he was near her, he forgot about the shooting and old scores and professionalism and rules—though he was admittedly never big on those, anyway. She made him forget his goals and purpose, something no one had done for a long, long time.

"You could run a small war from this room," he said in an effort to focus on the business at hand.

Jade glanced over her shoulder. Those intense green eyes focused briefly on his face. "We are. The bad guys want to take you out. We're not going to let them."

Direct. To the point. Where he knew the situation had layers of problems and complications—admittedly ones he hadn't completely shared with her—she broke things down to their most basic pieces. "Do you always see things so simply?"

"Mostly. I have a simple job."

He indicated the technology-strewn table with a sweep of his hand. "Seems pretty complex to me."

"That's because you still work for our blessed but flawed federal government." She shrugged and turned away. "David, you want to tell Mr. Tremaine what our job is?"

"Get them before they get you."

Remy laughed, moving around the table to sit across from them. "A good philosophy."

"It works for us," Jade said, frowning at him. "I thought you were going to get some rest."

"I tried, but I can't seem to relax. Probably too much caffeine."

Actually, every time he closed his eyes all he saw was the two of them naked and tangled in the sheets of his bed.

Her eyes heated for a moment—with anger or maybe the same desire simmering in his veins. Probably an reluctant combination of both.

"You really need to sleep."

"Trying to get rid of me?"

The *yes* was obviously on the tip of her tongue, but she swallowed it. "You're a big boy. Do what you want." She picked up an ammunition clip and checked it, adding, "You'll be here for the next few days anyway. Plenty of time to recuperate."

Even as he admired her I'll-slip-this-in-when-he-won't-notice strategy, he wasn't complying. "I don't think so, Agent Broussard."

"I'm not an agent, and you'll do what I say."

"I'll do what I please."

"Not if you want my team protecting you."

His body responded to her order by hardening like a rock. He wanted her when she was angry and defiant. He wanted her soft and vulnerable. Was there any situation where she couldn't—literally—get a rise out of him?

He did realize that forcing his point would get him nowhere. She'd never back down in front of her team.

"Could we discuss this in my office?" he asked as he rose.

"Office? You don't—"

"How about the room I'm currently sleeping and working in?"

She sighed—heavily. "David, continue to run the equipment diagnostics. Mo, keeping working on those names and background checks. I want the most likely suspect ASAP. I'll be right back."

She stalked toward Remy's bedroom door, crossed the threshold, then stood at the end of the bed with her feet planted shoulder-width apart, her hands braced on her hips. She looked as though she planned to go ten rounds with the heavyweight champ.

He was tense, as well. It was both heady and annoying to

have dreamed about being with her, to finally have her near him, only to have her constantly trying to distance herself.

But in contrast to her anger, he took great pains to move slowly, to close the door behind him with a quiet click and face her with a slight smile on his face. "Clients are a pain in the ass, huh?"

"Yes, they are."

"And yet without them, you wouldn't have a business."

She narrowed her eyes. "I have *agreeable* clients. Ones who listen to me, ones who don't question—"

"Ones who are too damn scared to do anything else."

She said nothing for several long moments. "I don't like you very much."

"What a shame. I like you very much." Before she could add another terse comment that might send his temper careening over the edge she'd already jumped off, he walked toward her, stopping when he was just inches away. "I'm not scared, Jade. At least not of getting shot again. I'm troubled by the need you rouse in me. I wonder if I'll forget what I'm here to do."

Instead of touching her, he should be finding a way to separate his fascination with her from his need for her investigative skills. There had been times he'd tossed aside professional ethics, but never for sex.

Ahem.

Okay, so there was that case in Boston years ago when he probably should have resisted the charms of that lovely blond secretary who worked for the drug cartel....

But that was just fun and games. This thing with Jade felt too intense to be a game. Fun...well, maybe...*if a man had the right touch.*

Thankfully—or not, depending on which parts of him he

asked—she didn't seem to give a damn about his confession of attraction. "We need to get the people on your suspect list under surveillance, and you're laying low for a couple of days while I gather resources and information."

"I can't do that."

"And I can't fight blind."

He had issues with being trapped—which was how he viewed holing up in a hotel room, luxurious or not. He knew this stemmed from his childhood days at the orphanage. While the nuns had been caring and gentle, his movements had been restricted to the convent; his choices had been limited. Had his foray into rebellion and eventual thievery been genetic or circumstantial? He'd likely never know for certain.

"I have to *do* something," he said.

"I'll put you to work."

"I work better in the field. You must realize I can get in and out of here without anyone knowing."

Her eyes flashed. "Not without *me* knowing."

"Jade, Jade…" He cupped her elbows. "I'm trying here. I'm really trying to work with you. But you can't put me in a box. You can't honestly expect I'd agree to that."

She pulled away, then paced in a circle before facing him again. "I'm *asking* you to stay put. Just a day or two. I need time to check with my network of contacts about your suspects. Two of them are all the way across the country in San Francisco and one is in south Florida."

He could help by giving her more information. But he'd promised himself to let her roll with this case her way. After all these years, if he'd made a mistake or jumped to the wrong conclusions, he might never have the answers he sought. "Do you ever stop pushing?"

"No."

He'd expected nothing less. Wasn't that why he'd hired her in the first place? "You're asking a lot."

"I'm doing what's necessary. You know I am."

He knew.

"Do you really intend to tell me everything about your past?" she asked. "The parts that aren't in your file?"

"Do you really intend to continue to deny our chemistry?"

She sighed and stepped back. "We're not getting anywhere."

They certainly weren't. But as much as he needed her to do her job, to make sure his own investigation had indeed led him in the right direction, he needed her touch, her kiss, her sighs of pleasure even more.

His muscles twitched with the effort of holding back. He clenched his fists at his sides and fought to control his breathing.

"There are parts of my life that aren't pretty," he said finally.

"I'm not denying our chemistry," she said at the same time.

She extended her hands. "You first."

"Ladies first. Besides, mine will take longer to tell."

She huffed out a breath. "Okay, look. We've got a personal issue with each other. I'm not completely immune, and *obviously* you're not."

Was that a compliment? He didn't think so.

"It's just something we're going to have to work around," she continued. "It's a chemical thing that pops up from time to time when men and women work together. Close quarters, tense moments, etcetera."

He loved her short, businesslike tone. He'd known her three hours, and yet he already realized it was so *her*. "Really? When was the last time it cropped up for you?"

"I don't think we need to go into specifics."

"Sure we do."

She sighed. "Okay, so maybe one time I let myself get too close to a target. The results weren't pretty, so you'd better—"

"He got killed?"

"Well, no, but—"

"He was injured?"

"Well, yes, but not because of anything I—"

"He just betrayed you by sneaking off with a terrorist—the one from whom he'd been accepting bribes for more than a year. Then he got shot, got scared and turned over evidence to your superior, who cut him a no-jail-time deal with the government."

She went still, her eyes frosting over. "Somebody's been doing some digging."

"Naturally." He reached out, trailing his finger along her cheek. "In fact, I know a great deal more about you than I imagine you're comfortable with."

"And yet you won't grant me the same courtesy."

"I'm getting around to it. I would just rather talk about the *personal issue* between us." His tone deepened as desire rolled through his stomach. "Exploring chemistry can be a healthy release."

"It can also be an unnecessary distraction."

"We'll set guidelines."

"I won't—"

"Consider it."

She licked her lips, drawing his gaze and forcing him to suppress a moan. "Okay."

He smiled, sliding his thumb across her bottom lip. "It's a start."

4

MAYBE IT WAS the probing, conflicted expression in Remy's eyes. Maybe it was simply time to give in to someone's opinions other than her own. Maybe she was just exhausted. But Jade was certainly tempted.

Foolish, definitely. But the lure was there, glimmering in front of her like an inviting respite from holding everything in, from doubting and fighting to stay in control. Even as he aggravated her, this man might equal her strength and challenge her as no one ever had before.

For now, though, she had to set it aside.

"We have a lot to talk about, but we don't have to do it now," she said, rolling her shoulders and stepping back. "I want to see what Mo comes up with. In the meantime, I'll find a way to let you out, but you have to keep out of sight. You're supposed to be a traumatized art dealer."

"Yes, ma'am." He grinned. "Boss. Chief."

"I prefer the last two."

"I figured."

"I gotta get some sleep. I'm getting punchy."

"Because you're tempted by me."

"Because I'm tired. I'll grill you later, don't worry."

"Promise?"

"Count on it."

"I don't suppose you'd let me tuck you in?"

She smiled wanly. "You supposed right." She headed toward the door. "But I'll be ready for the life and times of Remington Tremaine when I get up."

"You're giving me time to deal with my own demons, aren't you?"

She turned the doorknob but didn't look back. "Of course not. I'm just tired."

After leaving her client, she checked briefly on David and Mo, then shut herself in the guest bedroom.

Okay, maybe she *was* going soft. But then maybe she just needed a break from Tremaine's magnetism. He knew way too much about her. She probably should have expected his craftiness, but the day had had so many twists and turns it was no wonder she was dizzy. Not to mention she was out of practice with sophisticated intrigue.

Most of the people she defended her clients against these days were angry or overly devoted or just plain crazy. Plus, her primary goal was preventative protection, which involved an entirely different kind of smarts.

Closing her eyes as she lay back on the bed, she fought to put Tremaine out of her mind. He'd occupied every minute of her thoughts all day. She needed a break—along with a healthy dose of perspective.

Her partner, Frank, would be arriving soon. He'd help serve as a buffer between her and Tremaine. He'd have fresh ideas and the professional distance she couldn't seem to hold on to.

Was that why she'd put off her client's confession regarding his dodgy history? Was she so desperate for balance that she'd stalled receiving vital information? Or was she afraid she'd hear something that would push her irrevocably to either accept or reject him?

Before this case, her opinion of him had been anything but positive. Since she'd met him she'd budged little. But her conscience niggled. What if she was wrong about him? What if she'd sneered at a man who had value way beyond the shallow box she was determined to keep him in?

You're still thinking about him.

She mentally worked through cleaning and loading her pistol, hoping to bore herself to sleep. As she drifted, her parents' faces hovered before her.

She remembered her dad teaching her to change the beer tap and how to bluff at poker. He used to wear Old Spice cologne and would pull her into his lap during late-night card games, long after she was supposed to have been asleep.

She'd been a night owl even then.

She remembered her mom's perfectly manicured hands reflected in the mirror as Jade sat at her dressing table. Momma had liked Jade's hair—which she'd brushed and braided constantly—long. Once in high school, after they'd argued about her curfew, Jade had cut it off really short, and her mom had cried.

Jade had kept it long—though not waist-length—ever since. No doubt there was psychological funny business in that decision, some leftover sense of guilt for hurting her now-dead mother.

As always, her dream came back to that hot June day when a group of terrorists had decided to use a parade to assassinate the mayor of New Orleans. As grand marshal, her dad had been right beside him, her mother on the other side. The three of them, plus the mayor's bodyguard, had died in the shooting.

Jade hadn't been there. She'd been in calculus class at

Tulane. She hadn't said goodbye to them. She hadn't appreciated or loved them enough. And then they were gone.

The NSA had seen her pain and with stealth tactics and subtle training, turned it into controlled fury. At the tender age of nineteen, she'd started a new life of intrigue and danger—all in the name of revenge.

She jolted awake at the knock on the door.

Her hand automatically jerked to her holster as she sat up and blinked the dreams and the past away.

"J.B.?"

Frank.

"Coming."

She unlocked and opened the door, then immediately sank onto the end of the bed. She rarely dreamed, so the cobwebs were hard to bat away.

Her partner dropped onto the bed beside her. He wore his usual baggy jeans and button-down shirt—today, baby blue. His face was scruffy, and his sandy-brown hair looked as though he'd run his hands through it at least a thousand times.

But the crinkles spreading out from his dark-brown eyes betrayed his sharpness—if you took the time to look. He was only ten years older than her, but he had what people romantically refer to as an "old soul," so he acted more like her father than her brother.

"What's up with the locked door?" he asked.

"With Light-fingered Tremaine on the case, I figured the precaution was necessary."

Frank glanced at the door. "Not much of a lock."

"Don't I know it." She narrowed her eyes at him. "What the hell did you do last night? You look terrible."

"I reworked the Ace One security program."

"No kidding? You got the bugs out?"

"Yep."

All thoughts of sleep gone, she leaped to her feet. "You're a freakin' genius!"

"You had doubts before?"

"Did you tell Mo?" Mo had taught Frank—who'd been previously technologically challenged—everything he knew. She wasn't sure how thrilled his teacher was liable to be about his student excelling quite so thoroughly.

"Oh, yeah. I told him." Frank smiled. "He's pissed. We had fifty bucks on who'd break it first."

"Can we test it here?"

"You really think there's going to be a full-scale assault on the penthouse suite?"

"I'm not as worried about them getting *in* as I am about *him*—" she nodded toward the living room, where, presumably, their client was waiting "—getting *out*."

"Certainly a bigger issue. I'll get it installed. We can probably consider this a fairly definitive test."

"I can't think of a better situation."

"He's the best."

Curious, Jade angled her head. "You really think so?"

"Near as I can figure."

"You met him?"

"Slick."

"In spades. What did you find out research-wise?"

"More than you, I bet."

"Cute."

"You wanna put fifty on it?"

Recalling Tremaine's evasive answers and, worse, her reaction to him, she shook her head. "Not particularly."

"I think he considers me a rival for your affections."

"How do you figure that?" she asked casually, though sweat prickled at the small of her back.

"Just got that sense."

"How long have you been here?"

"Ten minutes."

She rolled her eyes. The man was a master. How could she forget? He'd taught her, after all.

There was no telling what Frank had gotten from Tremaine in ten minutes—added to what he'd researched. When he saw them together, he'd really get a troubling picture.

She'd already briefed her partner on the suspected cause of their client's shooting, so he'd dug much further back in Tremaine's life.

"Let's hear the dirt," she said.

"He's an orphan."

Despite preparing to be cynical, her heart stuttered. Guess the old money, vineyards and real estate he'd told Lucas about were part of his cover. "No kidding?"

"Mom dropped him off at a Catholic orphanage when he was six months old. Father's identity unknown—blank on the birth certificate. Tremaine was his mother's last name, and she died three months after dropping him off with the nuns."

She swallowed.

"Around the age of fifteen, an old family friend came to visit him. Tremaine met with him in private, then told the nuns that the man hadn't known his family, that he'd been mistaken about his identity.

"A few months later, he started sneaking out of the convent. He got caught a couple of times, and the nuns sent him to confession and counseling. At first, they figured he was out looking for drugs or alcohol, but others don't think so."

"Who'd you get this from?"

"One of the nuns."

Being raised Catholic, though she'd been lapsed for many years, Jade had a hard time picturing anybody grilling nuns. "She just offered all this up?"

"I smiled nicely."

"Ha."

"And memorized a Bible verse she wanted me to learn."

"You're kidding."

"Nope. Micah 2:1. It's a warning about devising wickedness. Truth is, without the black cape and funny hat, she was kinda cute."

"Stop." Jade held up her hand. "Oh, please stop."

Frank cleared his throat. "Anyway, I got the info. You wanna hear it, or not?"

"He was sneaking out at night."

"Right. Nobody really knows what he was doing during all these late-night outings—except maybe the priest in the confessional booth—since Tremaine refused to tell anyone. But then the forays stopped. Supposedly."

"Supposedly?"

"My opinion. I think he just stopped getting caught."

"Our thief was born."

"Makes sense. For the next year he was the model student. The day he turned eighteen, he packed his suitcase and headed out for parts unknown. The mail the nuns tried to send him came back."

Again, an odd, sinking feeling rolled through her stomach.

Like her—until she'd found Lucas—Tremaine had been alone in the world. "He never went back?"

"Oh, he went back. Brought a big freakin' check that entirely renovated the orphanage—big-screen TVs, PCs, video-game units, board games, building blocks, playground equipment, solid-wood bunk beds, freshly painted walls. The works."

"Profits from an excellent thief."

Frank shrugged. "Maybe. He refused to let them credit him as the benefactor."

Just as he'd refused to defend himself earlier. She shook aside her emotions and concentrated on facts. "So he wanted a low profile."

"But why go back at all?"

"They'd raised him," she said.

"Plenty of people are raised without being grateful."

Or aren't as appreciative as they should be. At least until it's too late. "A question to be probed."

"You've been around him longer. What do you think?"

Oh, boy. "Could be guilt or genuine affection."

"You lean toward…?"

She recalled the soft, persuasive feel of his lips on hers, the smile of invitation—and the blank look in his eyes when she'd questioned whether or not his money was tainted. For once, she went with her heart. "Affection. But where does the NSA come in?"

"No idea there. Not surprisingly, no one will go on record. There are just the rumors we've all heard before—he turned evidence against a bigger, thieving fish. As far as personal impressions go, a couple of agents acknowledged they worked with him, but they found him competent and secretive—just what you'd expect."

"You called the NSA directly?"

"No. Tipping our connection didn't seem wise at the moment. I talked to trusted, but retired, people."

Jade leaned back against the door. "So, who's this old family friend?"

"No idea. The good sisters claimed not to know, either."

"Claimed?"

"Their loyalty is with Tremaine."

"So we need to talk to him."

"You think he's really going to tell us what we need to know?"

"It's his life. He'd better."

She turned the doorknob, determined to face the inevitable sooner than later.

"Jade?"

Turning, she met Frank's gaze.

"Are you okay with this?"

"Of course."

"What about Lucas?"

She fought against the hurt lingering near her heart. Why didn't he just trust her to take care of things? "Did he call you?"

"He left me a message. He's worried about you."

I am, too. "I cut him out of this case. He's mad."

"He could help."

She clenched her fists. "You're not serious."

"He knows about the art world, the clientele. He's known Tremaine longer. Maybe he could give us a perspective we aren't seeing."

"He's my cousin."

"Doesn't mean he should be eliminated as an expert."

Though her instincts protested, she tried to focus on

Frank's words. She trusted him like no one else. "I need to think about that."

"Don't think long. I imagine this case is gonna move quick."

Another knock rattled the door.

When Jade opened it, David stuck his head inside. "The police are about to release the scene back to the restaurant. Do we want to check it out?"

"They're offering to let us?"

"Apparently Tremaine's name brings out the manners."

"Yeah." Mentally, Jade shifted priorities in her head. She figured they'd have to sneak by the police scene restrictions. "Yeah, we want to see it." She turned to her partner, who now stood behind her. "You and Mo stay here with Tremaine. David and I will go."

"Fine by me." He rubbed his hands together. "I want to install that security system."

"Are we going to get a big bill from the Marriott for seriously altering their room?"

"Humph. They'll never know we were here."

As Frank stalked from the room, Jade followed, shaking her head. Questioning a man's home improvement/computer skills was like questioning the strength of his libido.

In the living room, she found their client beside Mo, both of them sitting at the dining room table amongst the surveillance and computer equipment.

"See this button here?" Mo was saying as he held up a particularly sophisticated tracking device. "Press it and you get a GPS position, so—"

"Feel free to give away all our secrets," Jade said. As if Tremaine needed *another* specialty.

The men rose.

"Well, boss, he's one of us, right?" Mo said, his massive size contrasting sharply with his contrite expression. "I figured—"

"No, he's not." Her gaze flicked to Tremaine, who—naturally—smiled. "He's a client, not a member of this team."

"But you have to admit, I'm not your usual client," Tremaine said.

"You're unusual, all right. And that's not a compliment," she added when his grin widened. "Okay, people. We have a new development. The local cops are giving us an opportunity to check out the scene, so David and I will go."

"And me," Tremaine added.

"You'll stay here with Mo and Frank, order lunch from room service and pretend to be traumatized."

"A wonderfully humiliating picture, but, no, I won't."

Did the man live to annoy just *her,* or was it everyone who didn't let him run them over?

"I don't mind keeping an extra-sharp eye on him," David said.

Jade raised her eyebrows. "Do you usually keep a *less* than sharp eye on our clients?"

He flushed. "Ah, well, no."

Tremaine approached her, and her pulse immediately, embarrassingly, sped up. "Are you telling me if you'd been shot, you'd let somebody else examine the scene?"

He knew perfectly well she wouldn't.

"And you did promise you'd find a way to let me out."

"I was thinking of a stroll down to the lobby," she said incredulously, "not to the scene of your near death."

"I need your help," he said, staring down at her, "not for you to run my life."

The sincerity gleaming from his silver eyes made her instantly suspicious. This was an act for the crowd. He'd shift to ruthlessness without a qualm if it would facilitate getting *his* way.

"My team gets to vote on the direction of cases. Clients don't."

"Well, you're just going to have to make an exception this time, aren't you?"

"The team votes. Guys?"

Grumbling and mumbling ensued, all of which fell in Tremaine's favor.

"Fine. I know when I'm outnumbered." She forced her anger to the pit of her stomach. It was an ego thing, after all. She wanted her way, and the others didn't agree. She was arrogant, but not stupid. She knew Tremaine, unlike other clients, could handle himself, even though she knew she'd have to constantly remind him who was in charge.

"I don't like it." She crossed her arms over her chest and cocked her head. "But it's your funeral." She smiled.

"I was sort of hoping to avoid that."

"Mmm, well, Frank *has* gotten your signature on the standard security protection release, hasn't he?"

"I don't think so."

"He will before we leave." She turned back to the bedroom. She wanted to splash some water on her face. "Which we do in fifteen minutes."

5

REMY EXITED THE limo alongside Jade and David in front of Plush, the restaurant where he'd been shot.

The feelings of isolation and being locked in faded as he stepped onto the sidewalk. Power and confidence returned. He'd had to come back, he realized. Not just to forward the investigation, but to shed the sense of helplessness he'd been forced to embrace. The role he'd played that night had required him to swallow a huge part of himself—the warrior side.

They walked into the restaurant, which was obviously winding down from the lunchtime rush. As Jade approached the maître d', Remy started to intervene, but the man had obviously been forewarned about their arrival, because he frowned when he noticed Jade. "Ms. Broussard?"

"That's me."

"The detective is on the patio. Alone. We've been banned from allowing diners out there all day."

Jade shrugged, her head already turning toward the patio. "That's their decision, not mine."

"Yes, well." He spotted Remy. "*Mr. Tremaine.* Oh, *sir,* it's so good to see you up and about. We were so grateful you weren't seriously injured. We sent flowers to the hospital, but they said you'd already been released."

"Who said?" Jade asked abruptly, her head snapping around.

The maître d' blinked. "The person who answered the phone at the hospital."

"Did he give any other information?" she asked sharply.

"No." He looked to Remy and smiled. "But now you're here, so instead we'll serve you a wonderful lunch—on the house, of course."

Remy laid his hand on the maître d's shoulder. "Thank you so much, John, but I'm afraid I can't take the time today."

"But you *will* dine here again, sir, won't you?" he asked, almost desperately, as Remy turned away.

"You can count on it."

"At least the yahoos at the hospital didn't give out your home address," Jade said as they headed toward the patio.

"Probably because I didn't give it to them. But my office is easily known. I'd like to go there next."

"Not until after we do a bomb sweep."

"With all that equipment at the hotel, I'm sure you can arrange that without a problem."

"I'll be sure to put it on top of my list, *sir.*"

"You didn't honestly expect I'd sit by, did you?" he asked, well aware she was ticked he'd won their minor skirmish about his coming along.

"No, but I don't have to be happy about it, do I?"

"Ms. Broussard." A man with a crew cut and wire-rimmed glasses, dressed in khakis and a navy polo shirt approached them as they walked onto the patio. "I thought I recognized you getting out of the limo."

Jade shook his hand briefly. "Did you? I don't think we've met, Detective...."

"Parker. Your cousin Lucas and I have worked a few cases

together. He described you." His gaze dropped to her feet. "All the way down to your boots."

Jade smiled wanly. "He's efficient that way. This is Remington Tremaine and my associate, David Washington."

"We've been anxious to depose Mr. Tremaine. How convenient that he's here now."

His formal, polite tone was at odds with the demeanor of most cops Remy had come into contact with. A formality for him? Or rather for his art-dealer persona?

"We're an accommodating bunch," Jade said, her sarcasm apparently lost on the detective. "Why don't you do that while I look around?"

"Fine. Mr. Tremaine?" Parker extended his arm to indicate a two-seater table on the other side of the patio from where Remy had been shot. Remy sat opposite him while occasionally shooting glances at Jade, who'd knelt on the ground.

She ran her hand across a dark stain on the floor, where his blood had seeped into the concrete. He found the act strangely intimate. A shiver rolled through his body. What would have happened if she had been his date that night?

For one, he wouldn't have had to listen to inane chatter about hair and makeup tips for blondes.

Would she have reacted more quickly? Could she have apprehended the shooter? She certainly would have given chase, which he hadn't. He'd been so concerned about protecting his cover he'd done little but appear helpless.

At the hospital she would have been fierce and demanding. No bull, no PR quotes, no evasive answers. She'd fight for him. After being alone for so long, he liked the idea of a caretaker, of someone battling for him, alongside him.

He wished the two of them could have come to the scene

alone—which he'd planned to do after hours, under the comfortable cover of darkness. But that was before the police made their generous offer. Their generous, secret-agenda-attached offer.

During most of his cases, he found the local cops to be an inconvenience or an annoyance—though maybe that judgment was a holdover from his thieving days. Still, he recognized that for everyone else in the country they were the first line of defense against a dangerous, unpredictable world. They did a mostly thankless job for not near the compensation they deserved. So, he could stuff his uneasiness and arrogance—and, *be honest,* his guilt—for a few minutes.

"I understand Ms. Broussard is from New Orleans," Detective Parker said.

"Yes."

"Yet you live here."

Remy nodded, pretending he had no idea where Parker was going with his questions. "Yes."

"Her cousin is your attorney, who's also from New Orleans."

"I believe he had a law practice there at one time."

"Your birthplace is listed as San Francisco."

"Yes."

Parker's eyes narrowed. Obviously, he was frustrated that his leading questions were going nowhere. "How did you meet Jade and Lucas Broussard?"

"Lucas was recommended to me by a colleague some years ago. He, in turn, recommended Ms. Broussard for security services."

"You often require a bodyguard?"

"No. I require security services."

"As an art dealer."

"And businessman."

Parker was fishing with a long rod and the bait wasn't tempted enough to bite. Remy's public profile had been carefully crafted and filled in by the NSA. Maybe Parker sensed something wasn't completely right with Remy's bio, or maybe somebody higher up the chain of command had insisted on special treatment for him. Maybe Parker was simply curious about why Remy would hire a woman for his security detail. Whichever, the detective definitely wanted the scoop.

Not that he'd get it.

Parker laid a minirecorder on the table. "So, let's talk about the shooting two nights ago."

Remy responded to the interrogation and gave as detailed an account as he could recall. Though he was certain his case was beyond the local police, he gave as much information as he could. Anybody could break a case. A patrol cop, the chief of police or the owner of a delicatessen.

As he glanced beyond the patio to the sidewalk, he realized—again, as he had the night of the shooting—that the only thing separating the people on the street from the diners was a three-foot-high wrought-iron fence. Why had the would-be assassin chosen this spot, this time? There were way too many elements of chance to take into account and way too much risk.

During the questioning, he had a hard time focusing. He wanted to go to Jade. He wanted to kneel beside her and see what she saw, get her perspective.

But he wasn't supposed to know anything about blood-stains or shooting trajectories. This trade-off, this *lie* that enabled him to do his job, always bothered him. But he did it.

For the greater good? Or for his own protection?

When they finished, he and the detective walked over to David and Jade.

"What caliber weapon was used?" she asked, rising from a crouch as they approached.

"Nine millimeter. We found three shell casings." Parker pointed to the specific spots.

"What about photos?"

"Ah, they're at the station. I can't really…" He glanced nervously at Remy. "You could ask the captain."

"Yeah, I'll do that."

Remy could sense her annoyance, even if the detective couldn't. She wanted those case files. He could get them for her, but he sensed Jade's opinion of him would lower even further if he did. And while part of him wanted to mock her deep-rooted values and belief in truth and justice, the other part of him was humbled by her conviction and dedication.

"I'm getting nothing," she said, rolling her shoulders back. "No sense of why him, why now, why such a sloppy attempt. You, David?"

"Drive-by woulda been smarter," he said.

"Definitely. There's no good escape route." She pointed to the iron railing. "Too many people blocking the way to the target. Too easy for things to go wrong. Which they did."

The fact that their thoughts ran along the same lines bolstered Remy's opinion of her and her team. He knew they'd be thorough; he was glad they were smart, as well.

"You guys got any suspects?" Jade asked Parker.

"We're pursuing leads."

Translation: they had nothing.

"Maybe it was a random thing," Parker added.

"No way," Jade said. "The waiter's uniform, remember?

And if some guy wanted to just shoot into a crowd, he could have stood on the sidewalk and done it. He wouldn't have trapped himself inside the patio." She turned in a quick circle, then faced Remy. "Does being back help with any details for you? You remember any unusual sound or smell—something like that?"

Remy shook his head, equally frustrated by the unhelpful trip. "Nothing."

"Thank you for your time, Detective." She shook Parker's hand. "You'll let us know if you get any leads?"

"Sure. Where should I contact you?"

"The same number as before."

"And Mr. Tremaine, will he be home if we need him?"

Jade shook her head. "Just call the number." She turned and walked toward the restaurant. "Come on, guys."

Once in the limo, Jade directed the driver to the hotel.

"I need to go to my office," Remy said.

"You can go after the bomb sweep."

"I need to go now."

"Going before the bomb sweep is inadvisable."

"Can't you do that now?"

They sat on opposite ends of the backseat, with David facing them, his gaze flicking back and forth as if he were watching a tennis match.

"My team is working at full capacity. We'll get to your office as soon as possible."

"Today?"

"If possible. Let's go to the shooting range instead."

"And do what?"

"Pick flowers in the meadow."

"You actually like that, I guess."

"Picking flowers or shooting?"

"Guns."

"I don't like them, but my job requires me to be proficient with them. Plus, shooting at the range is a great way to release aggression safely." She angled her head. "You carry a gun. Surely you know how to fire it."

"Of course I know *how*. I just don't particularly enjoy doing it."

"You're not any good at it, are you?"

"Not really, no."

Her lips turned up at the corners in a half smile that was— graciously—only partly mocking. "Lucky for you, Tremaine, I'm an expert."

"So I hear."

Their gazes held for just a moment longer than necessary, leaving him to wonder what else they could teach each other.

She flicked the switch to talk to the driver and gave him the address of a popular downtown indoor gun club. She'd probably researched and memorized that before she'd gotten off the plane. But there was something stimulating about a take-charge woman who probably wouldn't need a weapon to kick your butt.

"Make yourself useful and call your maître d' buddy," she said. "See if you can get him to give you a list of everybody who ate in the restaurant that night."

"He won't be able to give us the people who paid cash."

"The average bill in that place is probably three hundred bucks. Nobody carries that kind of cash these days."

"Ahem."

She rolled her eyes. "No kidding? And here I had you figured for a black American Express."

"Ahem."

"Just make the call."

Remy's cell phone rang before he'd finished dialing the restaurant. "Yes?"

"Hey, Mr. Tremaine. It's Colin Hannigan. Heard you ran into some trouble the other night."

Even for Colin—a small-time criminal and sometimes informant for the government—he'd heard the news quickly. "You're certainly well-informed."

He felt, rather than saw, Jade sit up straighter at his words.

"Ha, ha," Colin said. "My job, right?"

"On occasion."

"The thing is…"

Remy could practically see the sweat roll down Colin's pale forehead.

"The thing is…" he said again. "I heard somethin' you might be interested in."

"Did you?"

"Yeah, well. I thought we might make our usual deal."

"We might."

Colin had helped in a minor way on a few cases, though Remy knew a few agents who used him more frequently. Colin was known to embellish facts or his importance in gathering info in order to get a better bribe—which he generally spent in a Vegas casino. The guy really ought to move out there, considering the money he'd save on airfare.

"Can we meet at Club Pi tonight, about ten?"

"I can arrange that."

"I'll be on the second level. You'll see me."

"Until then."

Remy flipped his phone closed. "We need to go to a club tonight."

Jade smirked. "Hot date?"

"With one of my semiregular informants. He may know something about my case."

"May?"

She would leap on that one word. "He has interesting information just over half the time."

"I'm not crazy about those odds, Tremaine."

"Me, either."

He also wondered how Colin could know anything about a crime that had actually begun thirty-five years ago.

Maybe Remy was wrong about the source of his trouble. Maybe he'd spent so long obsessing about the details and nuances of those long-ago events that he'd completely lost perspective.

There was certainly only one way to find out.

As Jade led Remy toward the shooting gallery at Masters Gun Club, she couldn't help the slight spring in her step. Finally, she'd found something she could best Mr. Superstar at.

"You'll use my pistol," she said. "That pea shooter you carry probably won't even penetrate the paper target."

He stopped, angling his head. "Are we actually comparing the size of our weapons?"

She looked him over. "You think you can measure up?"

Before she'd blinked, he'd pinned her against the wall, his body molded to the length of hers. "Oh, I think so."

His heat and desire enveloped her. Normally, her survival instincts would have been the first thing to kick in. But nothing was normal about this man. When she should have dropped him to his knees with a well-placed groin shot, she instead looked into his eyes and reveled in the hunger she saw there.

Her body pulsed; her skin tingled.

There was no talking herself out of wanting him. There was no pretending he didn't affect her as no man had in a very long time—maybe ever.

"Have you thought about setting guidelines for our chemistry experiment?" he asked.

Partly embarrassed that he made her lose control so easily and partly fascinated by her own unusual behavior, she licked her lips. "No."

He stroked his hand down her face. "I'm not much on patience."

She leaned into his warmth. "Neither am I."

"But…?"

"But we have a case."

"We'll always have cases."

"Not yours. You're a client. It isn't professional."

"Screw professional."

The whole, wild, unbelievable situation suddenly made her smile. It was either that or scream. "That's exactly what we're *not* supposed to be doing."

He hung his head. "You're killing me."

She took advantage of his relaxed position to duck under his arm. "I'm not supposed to be doing that, either." After she took a deep, bracing breath, she grabbed two pairs of earphones from the hooks on the wall. "Let's work out some of that frustration."

"I can think of much better ways to do that. And the only special equipment required comes in a small foil package." He grinned. "Which I have plenty of, by the way."

Shaking her head and ignoring the flip-flops of her heart, Jade put on the protective headgear, then opened the door to the hallway of shooting stalls.

No one else was firing, so she selected the first stall. Set up like a bowling alley, you could see all the targets, if not the other shooters. Complete concentration was essential.

How she was going to do that with the biggest distraction on the planet beside her, she had no idea.

As she pressed the button to send the target away from them along the overhead track, she tried to blank her mind. Having the hots for a client was bad enough, but if she shot badly, she'd never live it down.

Target in place, she checked her ammunition clip and took her stance as she narrowed her eyes at the notch at the end of her pistol and aimed some fifty yards away. She didn't flinch as the gun recoiled. In fact, she barely moved at all as she unloaded nine quick rounds.

Tremaine said nothing as she flipped the switch to bring the target back. She didn't, either, knowing her results would speak for themselves. She never bragged about her skills on the firing range. But the man beside her brought out her competitive edge.

Among other things.

His eyes widened as the target reached them. Every shot was so dead center there were only five holes in the paper. "Your reputation isn't an exaggeration," he said loudly so she could hear him through the headphones.

The Arrow. Jade nearly rolled her eyes. Couldn't they have come up with a cooler moniker? Such as former colleague Butch Pelion, a detonation expert who was known as "Smoke." *That* was a great nickname.

She reloaded the gun, then handed it to Remy. "You next."

As he took his stance and fired, she watched him closely. He had nice posture and balanced well—not surprising, given his former profession—but he held his arms too stiffly and clenched his hands around the weapon. It was a mistake she'd seen often when a shooter was fighting the recoil with his hands rather than his shoulders.

The holes in the target reflected his tension. He had a few that were reasonably center, but others were wildly off.

After replacing the target, she stood behind him, laying her arms along the outside of his. Since he was taller, he had to crouch a bit for her to reach him. "Pin your shoulders down," she said loudly. "Absorb the impact there, not in your hands. Don't lock your elbows."

He nodded and settled his shoulders.

"Better." She moved around him and laid her hands over his. "Don't be so stiff here. There's a difference between tight and stiff. Keep your fingers nimble."

Being so close to him was necessary for teaching, but made her stomach tremble and sweat roll down her back. Why did he have to smell so amazing all the time?

"Don't hold it like you're afraid of it."

He turned his head, irritation sparking in his eyes. "I'm not."

Their faces were in dangerous proximity. And as their attraction bubbled beneath the surface, she could feel the level of competition rise. He'd had a fine ol' time breaking into her room and sneaking up on her while she was sleeping. He enjoyed rattling her with his secret smiles and ambivalent answers to her questions. He relished stepping into her personal space.

Needless to say, she was enjoying his current frustration a bit. She stepped back. "Show me."

He emptied the clip into the target again, and this time the results were better. They took turns after that, and either by her tips or his need to move closer to her level, he improved greatly.

On their way out, he wrapped his arm around her shoulders, the way a buddy, not a potential lover, would. "Thanks."

The fact that she was becoming used to him touching her, that he was somehow familiar after meeting him less than twenty-four hours ago said something about their chemistry. Or else she'd lost her mind.

"You were right," he added. "I enjoyed that. What's next?"

With true regret, she said, "Something you probably won't like."

BACK AT THE HOTEL, Jade organized her team.

She called the front desk and reserved the connecting room, then sent David in there to sleep, so he'd be refreshed for the night shift. She updated Frank on the call from informant Colin Hannigan, asked him to contact the police captain about the case file, then she sent him and Mo to Tremaine's office to do the sweep.

Before Mo left, though, he gave her a rundown on the suspects—where they were now and the resources needed to track their movements. He was certain of one thing—the shooting was a hired hit. The top three suspects were sophisticated, wealthy men who weren't likely to be seen dressing in waiter's uniforms and skulking around restaurants.

At one time or another, they had all dealt with the police on burglary or smuggling suspicions. They'd all skated by.

Other than that, Mo was hitting walls. His sense was that their client had more information than he was giving, confirming Jade's suspicion that Tremaine had more than one agenda on his mind.

With her team occupied, she gave herself the most arduous

task—getting the truth from their client. But first, she had to address tonight's meeting.

"I don't like the place where we're meeting the informant," she said, pacing in front of the sofa where Tremaine sat.

"It's a crowded nightclub—very public. I've been there before, so I can give you the layout."

"Like the restaurant was public."

"But this time you'll be there to protect me."

She shook her head at him. "You think you're cute, but you're not."

"I am, in fact, adorable." He paused, his eyes sparkling. "When the situation calls for it."

She didn't even have to look over to know he was smiling. "I have no doubt."

"Why are you always moving and talking at the same time?"

"It helps me think better."

"Looks to me like you're running. Possibly away from something."

"Stuff your psychology and tell me more about Colin, the informant."

"I think you're running from your feelings for me."

Now she did stop. She planted her hands on her hips and turned toward him. "My *feelings* for you? You have lost your mind."

"I don't think so. You're afraid to give in to your attraction to me."

She reminded herself he was good at pushing buttons. Was he trying to get her off topic? Was this his ego talking? Was he worried about how an attraction might affect his case? Or did he honestly care how she felt?

Probably some combination of all of the above.

"I'm not afraid of anything, and whatever sparks are between us will be ignored during this case."

"That's not possible for me."

"Oh, please. You're a professional."

"It's not going to go away just because you deem it so."

"Yes, it will."

He said nothing for a long moment. He simply stared at her. "Have you really shut yourself so completely off from your feelings?" he finally asked quietly.

She followed her own advice and ignored the quivering in her belly. In fact, instead of softening her, his question made her angry.

With all of his secrets and personal agendas, he had the nerve to critique her. "Okay, let's set aside the relatively unimportant issue of talking about the latest development in your case, and let's talk about *feelings*. And motivations behind feelings. You, for instance. Why did you hire my cousin as your attorney? You *just happened* to be in my bar, and he *just happened* to be there and you two *just happened* to talk shop?"

The smile had fallen away from his face, but his direct gaze never wavered. "I was curious about you."

"Me?" The shocked response slipped out before she'd thought to edit it. The idea that he'd secretly sought her out did strange things to her heart rate. "So you used my cousin to snoop around my private life."

"Yes."

She took a slow breath, then blew it out even slower. She was both annoyed and flattered. "Why?"

"I found you fascinating."

Holy hell.

"Still do, actually."

Her heart pounded harder. "You mean like a professional curiosity thing, or…"

"There's a bit of that. But mostly I have a wild crush on you. I think you're beautiful and interesting. Your talents intrigue me, and your body distracts me."

Only years of training kept her on her feet. He'd literally weakened her knees. "Why are you telling me this now?"

"I have to start trusting you sometime."

She tried to find her cynicism. It was either that or melt into the carpet. "As much as you can, anyway."

He smiled. "Exactly. And I am leading to a point. For a long time now, I've wanted to know what drove a woman so young into the arms of the NSA."

Was the heated look in his eyes all about their chemistry or did she detect a hint of anger? "I guess you found out."

"They took advantage of your grief and used your rage and pain for their own purposes. I find that despicable."

She fisted her hands against their trembling. The idea that she might have had a champion, a defender to protect her from the NSA—the people who'd both given her what she wanted, yet withheld what she really needed—sent a wave of comfort washing over her.

She'd been alone. She hadn't known Lucas existed at that time. All she'd had was her hatred and fury.

Part of her wouldn't change anything. If presented with the same decision today, she'd undoubtedly make the same choice. Though she'd lost her chance to be normal and the violence and deceit had preyed upon her psyche, she'd honored and avenged her family.

Her heart, along with her knees, softened at his righteous anger.

She cleared her throat. "I did what I wanted. I was only nineteen, but I knew what they were doing."

"You realized after they trained you what they were doing."

"Maybe. But I knew from the first there was a catch." She shrugged. "It was worth it."

"Yes, I imagine it was. Revenge is a powerful emotion."

She had the feeling the point had arrived. "You know who's after you, don't you?"

"I think so."

"Dammit, Tremaine, you might have told me before I sent my team running around in circles."

"I needed to be sure I was right—for obvious reasons. I wanted you to double-check me. I still need you to do that. But I will tell you my suspicions."

For a second, Jade actually hesitated. The more she was with this man, the more she learned about him, the closer she could feel herself drawing to him. She didn't *want* to be closer to him.

No, that wasn't completely honest. She *shouldn't* be closer to him.

She'd made a critical mistake once before with a client. The results hadn't been pretty. While she hadn't crawled into bed with Senator Kilpatrick, she'd certainly let his stories of persecution and misunderstanding sway her emotions.

And he'd rewarded her with betrayal and humiliation.

"Jade?"

She crossed to the sofa and dropped next to him. "You think you've got more drama than me?" She waggled her fingers in a come-on gesture. "Let's hear it."

Naturally, he smiled.

6

"FOUR MONTHS AGO," Remy began, "a man called me and offered me money for a family heirloom."

"How much money?"

"A hundred thousand dollars."

She whistled. "Who was the man?"

Though the information he was about to reveal was important to his case, he also recognized that he wanted Jade to know him. Not the rumors or the outright lies. The real deal.

Or as real as he could be.

It didn't seem to matter that the timing was lousy, that being surrounded by security guards, cops and colleagues made their attraction awkward. His instincts screamed that this thing between them wasn't just physical.

Some part of her called to him. Was it the loneliness she tried to cover with aggression? Was it her quiet competence? Was it her strong character? Of her lack of patience for anything or anyone lacking in honor?

Or did he simply admire the way she'd taken her life in her own hands and made it into what she needed, even when fate had handed her pain and disaster?

"Peter Garner."

She narrowed her eyes, obviously remembering the name from his suspect list. "The art historian and dealer in San

Francisco. You were raised there. Did you know him grow-ing up?"

"No. I know him because I think he was responsible for the death of a family friend."

"Responsible?"

"He either murdered him, or had one of his employees do so."

"Who was the friend?"

"His name was Sean Nagel. He was a thief and not a par-ticularly good one, since he was convicted of burglary several times in his life."

"Clearly he didn't teach you."

Her dry comment cheered him. Her moral stand on his former profession was a big obstacle between them. If he ever expected to explore their attraction, they had to find some middle ground there.

"No, he certainly didn't. But he once came to see me and asked for the same heirloom. He said it belonged to him."

"Ah."

"Garner's phone call was definitely a lightbulb moment. I've spent the last twenty years of my life trying to get definitive proof of who killed Nagel, and why the heirloom is so important."

"And instead of a hundred thousand dollars, you get shot."

"It certainly looks that way."

"Is the heirloom worth that much?"

"I don't see how. It's a silver signet ring with an onyx stone in the center."

Jade angled her head. "This old family friend…Sean Nagel…"

Remy stiffened. *Was* he a friend? He remembered the coldness, the emptiness he'd seen in the man as he'd stared at him from across the table.

"He came to see you at the orphanage when you were fifteen," she continued. "You told the nuns that he hadn't known your family." Her eyes widened. "You lied to *nuns?*"

"I see Frank has been digging." But then he hadn't found out anything more than he should know. "And I didn't lie. Sister Mary Katherine sat right beside me during the meeting. She thought Nagel was a *hoodlum,* and she was the one who came up with the story to tell everyone else."

"Smart lady. So, how are Nagel, Garner, you and this ring connected?"

"I'm not sure." He suspected, but he hesitated in telling everything. He wanted Jade and her team to focus on the facts and let the investigation flow from there.

"You're all thieves," she said, watching him closely. "Or, at least, once were."

"Garner still is. He has an extensive smuggling-and-burglary operation that includes selling stolen property."

"Did you ever run into him when you were stealing?"

"Several times. We each knew what the other was doing, but we played word games and danced around admitting anything. And, of course, I've kept close tabs on him and the other two men on my suspect list for many years."

"But you never found any proof that he killed Nagel."

"No."

"You said the ring was a family heirloom. Who did it originally belong to?"

"My father."

"There's no father's name listed on your birth certificate."

Oh yeah, Frank had dug deep. "No, there isn't." He linked his hands, not wanting to go back, but knowing he had to. "You obviously know that when I was six months old my mother dropped me off at the orphanage and said she couldn't care for me by herself.

"She was a struggling waitress," he continued, "without any living relatives that I ever found. She'd obviously been abandoned by my father. That alone might have been enough to cause a young woman to give up her child to what she supposed would be a better life.

"And I flourished within the orphanage. I made friends easily, and I was quick in school. Very early on, I realized my ticket to freedom was my brain."

"Not your smile?" she asked in mock surprise.

He grinned. "That came later. For a while, I studied hard and kept in good favor with the sisters. Until Nagel came to see me and opened up my past. After that I was even more intrigued by the ring that was my only link to my nameless father. I wanted some answers."

"And the nuns weren't giving them."

"I don't think they knew any more than I did, but they refused to let me investigate."

"Let me guess…you didn't bide your time quietly in your room like a good altar boy and wait until they booted you out at eighteen to start snooping."

He liked that she understood him so well already. She may not like him, or what she'd hear, but she'd know. And, hopefully, accept. "No, I certainly didn't. And the stakes were raised significantly when Nagel was murdered near the waterfront, three days after visiting me."

She jolted. "Three days?"

"His visit to me had triggered something ugly in his life. As you can imagine, Sister Mary Katherine was even more adamant that I wasn't to get involved. She kept insisting to me that it was a case of mistaken identity, that he wasn't a family friend."

Jade frowned. "But the ring. You *did* have it. Clearly he knew something about you, about where—or who—you came from."

"I thought so, too. But Sister Mary Katherine had no intention of letting her prize student get involved in a murder mystery. So I started sneaking out at night."

Jade rolled her eyes, but he thought he detected a touch of affection in the gesture. "Naturally."

He continued his story by explaining to her about the library at the local university, which was open twenty-four hours to accommodate students. He'd taken advantage and begun his very first investigation there. At first, he'd learned very little. The police inquiry went nowhere, and nobody seemed to care that former felon Sean Nagel had died. He was divorced, listed in the obits as having no children, and his ex-wife certainly wasn't Remy's mother.

Remy's research into the ring hadn't gone any smoother. Though he'd found similarly designed rings in books about antiques, the one he had was clearly a cheap imitation. He'd been distracted and enthralled by those books about antiques. He'd moved on to paintings, sculptures and jewelry. He'd been fascinated by their history and beauty and vowed he'd own such wonderful works someday himself.

And the allure of being out at night on his own, released from the comforting bubble where he'd lived and in control of his destiny for the first time in his life, was more exciting than he'd anticipated.

"I loved the freedom, the darkness, even the danger that lurked on the streets."

"When did you start stealing?"

Trust Jade to call it what it was. "I ran with a gang of other boys my age for a while. They fooled around with vandalism. A couple of them were into drugs. But I'd been raised on the certainty of the fires of hell, so I kept myself clean.

"Until I learned my friend John's father beat him. He longed to escape, but was too frightened and too poor to try. One day, the father found John and me playing cards on the street corner. He snatched him by the arm, and the terror in John's eyes as he looked at the man who'd fathered him tore me to pieces. I tried to intervene, and got punched in the face for my efforts. But before he dragged John away, I swiped his watch. Which turned out to be a Rolex. I have no idea if his father had money he kept from his family, or if he'd stolen it himself, but it financed John's escape to L.A."

He watched her face closely for a reaction—a judgment—but she simply looked at him in return.

"It was so *easy*," he continued. "I took what I wanted, gave it to someone who needed it. My skill improved, and it became more natural. Did I know it was wrong? Of course. And yet…I convinced myself I was balancing the scales of injustice. I was redistributing things to those who needed them more."

She smirked. "Like Robin Hood?"

"So I fancied myself. I don't regret most of what I did. Maybe I should. Maybe someday I will." He shook aside any lingering remorse for those he had wronged and the deep-seated worry about why he'd turned to crime in the first place. He'd been young, arrogant and foolish at times, but he'd convinced himself he was in the right. He couldn't do it over. "I did what I thought should be done. I stole and gave. Occasionally, I stole and kept.

"I became a successful art dealer—both legitimate and not. I worked in museums and galleries to further my interest and education. I even dipped briefly into designing security systems."

Her jaw tensed as her eyes narrowed. "So you could break in later."

"Not at all. I never took from friends, Jade. I know that seems like a strange code to live by, but that's what I did. To admit all, however, I must say it began because my boss caught me breaking into his gallery. I wasn't doing it to steal anything. I'd simply forgotten my briefcase."

"So, instead of calling someone and asking for help, you broke in."

"Well, it wasn't that difficult, and in the end, I saved everybody a lot of time and money. I told my boss I'd found security breaches and thought I'd see what happened if I tried to break in. The story worked, he laughed about it with his high-dollar friends, and I eventually helped many of them with their own security issues." He angled his head, an idea he'd never considered suddenly occurring to him. "Maybe I was destined for law enforcement after all."

"You just think like a criminal. That's why it was easy for you to break in."

"Well, yes, but isn't that what you do?"

"All the time. When I'm working venue security I always look at the place as if I'm on the outside looking in, as if I'm raging angry with somebody and *have* to get to him." Her gaze cut his way. "Though it's easier with some clients than others."

"Then you'll be happy to hear my securities career came to an end as computers became more complicated. I've never really had the knack for that. I prefer something more hands-on."

"Like a lock pick."

He smiled. She really was coming to understand him. "Exactly."

"Did you really try to steal the Crown Jewels?"

"Good God, no. Too high profile. And what would I do with them? Wear them? Sell them?" He shook his head. "Way too hot." He leaned toward her and trailed his finger down her nose. "Though sometimes hot can be good."

She crossed her arms over her chest. "Don't try to distract me now. I bet you're just getting to the good parts."

The parts that were left didn't get good. They got worse.

He stood and crossed the room, staring out the window onto the vibrant, fast-moving city below. "Do you believe life runs in a circle?"

"Seems to runs in a line to me. You're born, you live, you die."

"Not for me. I've had many lives. Most of them pushed below the surface. It was fine for me. I liked living on the edge. But sometimes the things you do circle back. Like karma, if you believe in that sort of thing.

"My old friend John—the one I'd helped escape from his father—had always lived life by the book the way you do. Since moving to L.A. he'd made himself into a successful lawyer. An assistant district attorney."

"*You're* friends with a D.A.?"

"I was. He was gunned down outside his office four years ago."

Behind him, he heard her suck in a breath. Then, quietly, she said, "You joined the NSA almost four years ago."

"Yes. My past was suddenly my present. The ugliness I'd transformed into success seemed dirty again. I was convinced he was killed because of me, because he was one of few people I'd kept in touch with through both my legitimate and illegitimate careers. I had had lunch with him the day before. Had one of my old enemies seen us together? Had the past I'd so carefully covered somehow been brought into the light?"

"He was a D.A."

"I know. It could have been anyone. And it turned out to be a gang retaliation. But initially, there were no leads. So, because of my guilt, I made a terrible mistake." He shook his head, amazed still at his stupidity and brashness. "I went to the police for help."

"And they dug into your past."

He still remembered the moment he'd faced the stone-cold FBI agents and contemplated the fear of losing everything he'd worked and sacrificed for. He'd broken the law, and now his sins were coming around to bite him. Jade—along with the nuns— would have said it was justice. Instead, he'd felt betrayed. "They didn't know everything, but they'd found some coincidence of places I'd been when certain items had gone missing. They knew a little, and suspected a whole lot more."

"So they offered you a deal—prosecution or using your unique services for the good of your country."

"Yes."

"And now the past is coming back again."

"It seems so."

"Nagel still doesn't rest in peace, a murderer is still out there, but you still have the ring."

He nodded.

"With you?"

He didn't even pause as he lied. "No."

"But you can get to it."

"Yes."

She sighed, obviously sensing he wasn't going to give up its location. "So we start with Nagel and work our way forward. We continue our investigation into your shooting. Maybe we'll find a way to meet in the middle."

He finally turned from the window to face her. "About us, too?"

JADE FOUGHT TO focus on her *client*, not the *man* before her.

The *client* was just something to be protected. Like a vase or a building. The *man* had faults and weaknesses, admirable qualities and deep wells of strengths, intelligence and loyalties.

She'd expected to be repelled by his past. She'd expected to disagree with his every decision and choice. And while his path certainly wouldn't have been the one she'd choose, she admired him on some level.

A dangerous opinion for the compassionate woman who lurked beneath the unemotional, professional bodyguard.

"I'm solving your case," she said as she stood.

"And that's all?"

"We shouldn't—"

He shook his head. "Regrets come later." He walked toward her, his gait as smooth and elegant as ever. Now that she knew the struggle behind it, she appreciated his movements even more. "Don't think about should or shouldn't. What do you *want?*"

She wanted him. Too much. She tried to tell herself she didn't like or respect him. She fought to remind herself she was doing her job, then heading home as quickly as possible. She tried to regain the resentment she'd felt when Lucas had first said Tremaine's name.

Instead, she felt heat and need. Compassion and curiosity. How was she supposed to fight that? "I want to know why you hired me. Because I'm good at my job, or because of your, uh…"

"Crush?"

She felt her face heat.

His gaze intense, he cupped her jaw. "What do you think?"

The security box beside the suite door beeped twice. Jade stepped away from Tremaine just before the door flew open.

Frank and Mo strode through the opening. "Okay, people, the office is clear." They both stopped as they spotted Jade and Remy. "Problem?"

"No." Jade shoved her hands in the back pockets of her jeans. "We were just going over the case details. You got the surveillance in place?"

"It's set." Frank held up a small device that looked like a PDA. "We'll know if anybody gets in."

"Like an alarm?" Tremaine asked.

"One only we can detect here, though."

"So, if somebody breaks in…" Tremaine took a protesting step forward. "I have a lot of valuables in my office—"

"We'll get those," Frank said. "Can we take him, J.B.?"

"Now's as good a time as any," she said. She assumed Frank would explain that they wanted to know when or if somebody broke in, and they didn't want that person scared away by an alarm. But with the signet ring being such a key to the case, she needed to make sure it was secure.

"I need to talk to you a sec before you leave," she said to Tremaine.

"I've got phone calls to return," Frank said, heading toward the dining room.

Mo shrugged. "What've we got to eat?" He headed to the kitchen, presumably to find out.

"The ring is in your office?" she asked when she was alone with her client.

"No."

"But it's secure."

"Yes."

The resentment she'd longed for a few minutes earlier finally arrived. "Do you think I could actually see it?"

"I'll see what I can do."

"How gracious of you. Is Colin Hannigan an employee of Peter Garner?"

"Not as far as I know. He's a government informant."

"You think Garner knows about the NSA?"

"I don't see how, but anything is possible."

"And yet Hannigan has information about the shooting." She thought it was very likely Garner had found a connection between Tremaine and Hannigan—even if he didn't know the basis of the relationship—and had decided to use him in some way.

The links between past and present were varied. What had been the relationship between Garner and Nagel? Maybe boss and employee?

Had Garner known Remy owned the ring all this time? If so, why had he just now decided to get it back? When offering to buy it hadn't worked, why had he tried to shoot him? A warning?

"As for this meeting with your informant," she continued to Tremaine, "I still don't like it, but we're going."

"We?"

"You, too. You might be a rebellious troublemaker, but you're no fool."

He simply nodded. "Thank you."

"I'd like everything you can give me on Hannigan. And I'm going to ask around on my own today. All right?"

"That's fine. Thanks for letting me know."

"I appreciate you sharing your history. I know it wasn't easy."

"You needed to know."

"Yeah." Despite her resistance, they'd become more than guard and client in the past few hours, and she was uncertain how to move forward. Investigating the crime could easily take a backseat to investigating the man and her feelings toward him.

She needed to stay on track. His life was in danger, and he was counting on her to get him through safely.

"You ready, Tremaine?" Frank called from the other side of the room.

"Sure."

As he started to walk away, Jade grabbed his wrist. She cleared her throat as she looked up at him. "Remy, I'm sorry."

His eyes warmed at her use of his first name. "For what?"

"The loss of Nagel, your friend John and your parents."

His mouth lifted at the corners in a sexy smile that she was quickly becoming addicted to. "You, too."

During the limo ride to the club that night, Remy only half listened to Jade snap out orders about procedure and safety.

"…if *anything* makes you feel odd or uneasy, signal me right away. Don't go through large crowds unnecessarily. If you need to go to the bathroom…"

It was difficult to concentrate on her words, as she'd decided to let David and Frank be the security guards while she posed as his date. Which had some definite benefits for him.

She wore a short, halter-top dress in turquoise that revealed curves and lifted cleavage. She'd styled her shoulder-length red hair in soft waves, applied makeup that accentuated her eyes and added gloss to her lips.

He'd been fascinated with her lips since he'd first seen her. They'd softened against his when he'd managed to catch her off guard, though she drew them into a stern line most of the time. But with the shiny pink color highlighting them, they even looked appealing giving orders.

His life was on the line, and all he could think about were the magical things he could do to those lips, not to mention the pleasure they could bring him. He envisioned her trailing kisses across his chest, her tongue flicking out to taste his nipple.

Her mouth would venture lower, across the planes of his stomach, her hair trailing behind her and caressing his skin. His erection throbbed as she grew closer. He longed for that first touch, the first stroke of complete intimacy. He knew they'd be amazing together. If he could just convince her.

And get rid of the psycho trying to shoot him.

"Are you listening to me?"

He blinked out of his fantasy. "Absolutely."

She narrowed her eyes in suspicion, but continued. "Don't draw undue attention to yourself. Watch faces. Try to remember if you've seen them before...."

Where was I?

Oh, yeah, her lips pressed to my stomach....

His body pulsed in anticipation. He could smell her clean, simple scent, like fresh laundry or a summer breeze. He tangled his hand in her hair and closed his eyes. He could feel her breath against his skin, her hands kneading his thighs.

"Tremaine!"

A few hours ago it was Remy. If she was on the verge of giving him a blow job *surely* it would be Remy.

"Are you listening to me?" she asked.

My pants are way too tight, but yes, I hear you.

"I'm here," he said finally, trying to mentally dress himself as well as her.

"I get the sense that I don't have your full attention."

"You do." *Just not the attention you're probably interested in at the moment.*

"Have I explained that I don't like this meeting?"

"Several times."

"Are you going to actually follow directions?"

"I'll try."

Those glossy lips thinned. "Try hard."

"Yes, ma'am."

"And don't be cute."

"That'll take more effort."

"I'm sure. Are you armed?"

"Yes. Ankle holster. Are you?"

"Of course."

His gaze slid down her skimpy outfit. "Where?"

"Upper thigh, knife sleeve."

In a combination of pleasure and pain envisioning that, he closed his eyes briefly. "How did I miss you putting that on?"

She glanced at Frank and David, sitting across from them but engrossed in a handheld video game. "I'm not hiking up my dress for you, Tremaine," she said quietly.

"Maybe later?"

"Don't hold your breath."

He trailed his finger along her thigh. "How about I make you lose your breath instead?"

"We're working here, Tremaine."

"Back to *Tremaine,* are we? And we were making so much progress."

She cast another wary glance at her staff members, who were now arguing about the game. "I need to reestablish some distance. It's important that I stay objective."

"You can do your job and still like me."

"I can't let my emotions get involved."

"Emotions are always involved."

"Not for me."

He didn't believe her. In fact, he was pretty certain she felt things more deeply than most people. The dramatic losses in her life had forced her to cover up her softer side. "You don't feel compassion for your clients? You don't understand their fear and uncertainty?"

She crossed her arms over her chest. "For a man who's not good at answering questions, you ask some pretty nosey ones."

"I'm just trying to soften you up so I can have my wicked way with you."

"Then what?"

"I'm not big on smoking. How about a nice, long nap?"

"I'm serious."

"You think I'm not?"

"We live in different cities and have very different lives. I don't want to get involved with anybody now."

He could live anywhere. He'd simply chosen Atlanta for its size and sense of anonymity. "Hmm. Well, I did promise you guidelines, didn't I? I'm fine with a wild, temporary affair," he said, though as soon as the teasing words were out, he doubted them.

Was this attraction to her really all about sex? Was his need to be with her just curiosity about his long-time crush or a product of the tailspin his life had turned into? Did he need her for only advice and security, her expertise and understanding?

Or was there something more?

"I can't believe I'm considering this," she said, shaking her head.

"Take your time." He grinned. "On second thought, hurry up. In fact—" he looked at his watch "—if we can get through this meeting quickly, the night will still be young."

"Yeah? My calendar's pretty full protecting your backside."

"And think how much more intimately you could—"

"Hey, J.B.," Frank said. "Didn't you bust six million points on Hard Target?"

Remy forced himself to focus on Frank's question and stow his personal issues.

"Yes," Jade said, "but you guys are never going to match it on that little thing."

David frowned over the handheld game.

"You need the big game back at the office," she continued. "The gun attachment gives you a lot more control than the buttons on the minigame."

"I sense an office rivalry," Remy said, knowing Jade was grateful to be distracted by anything other than them. He'd concede the subject for now, but he had no intention of giving up.

"We have an arcade-size game, complete with plastic pistols, set up in the shooting range at the office. It's great for practice without expending ammo."

He raised his eyebrows. "You have your own indoor shooting range?"

"Oh, yeah," Frank said. "J.B. and I are big on keeping the

reflexes sharp, plus, we set up a side business, giving shooting lessons. It pays the bills when there's no mortal danger to protect people from."

"We mostly get cops or federal agents who want to improve their marksman skills," she said. "We found David that way."

"She's trying to gently point out that I suck at firearms," David said.

"Suck*ed*," Jade corrected.

"He was in the NOPD police academy," Frank said. "Great in every area."

"But I was a lousy marksman," David put in.

"J.B. and I got hold of him, improved his skills, then convinced him to give up his cop dreams and join us."

"Less bureaucracy," Jade said.

"And more action," David finished.

They high-fived across the seat.

If Remy had ever doubted the quality of the operation he'd entrusted his life to, this moment would have changed his mind. Jade and Frank's team respected and believed in them. So much of their leadership shined through the people who weren't in charge.

He also liked watching Jade and Frank together. Their father/daughter-like relationship had no doubt kept them both grounded during their years in the NSA. Part of him longed for the sense of teamwork and camaraderie at Williams-Broussard Investigations, even though he knew he was a loner.

Not since his days at the orphanage had he truly felt part of a special community. But Jade and her crew made him feel like a vital part of a cohesive, supportive unit. And while he'd tried to downplay the issue of his life being threatened, he could silently acknowledge that he valued their support.

They'd spent the afternoon studying pictures of Garner and his known associates, calling contacts in San Francisco to put him under surveillance and strategizing about his next possible move. Remy had done the same thing over the last couple of months, but now that the stakes had been raised considerably, he was grateful for the added resources of Jade's team.

"We're nearly there, J.B.," said a voice over the limo intercom.

Jade pressed a button near the door. "Thanks, Charlie."

"Another one of yours?" Remy asked.

"Would I trust your safety to anybody but the best?"

"No," Frank and David answered at the same time.

The relaxed, friendly mood lasted until they pulled up to the rear entrance of Club Pi. Remy wished he could buy the team drinks as a thank-you but doubted they'd agree to the indulgence. Maybe when all this was over.

Flanked by David and Frank, he and Jade joined hands and were hustled through the club's back door and into the kitchen. He cast a glance at the waiters and bar staff, who were giving them curious looks. "I feel so Hollywood."

"Just stay close to me and don't sign any autographs," Jade said, keeping a tight hold on his hand.

Remy tried to focus on the faces around him. He was supposed to absorb his surroundings. *Somebody* was certainly out to get him. Somebody most likely hired by Peter Garner, whom nobody would mistake for being a less-than-dangerous guy.

Self-preservation should be foremost in his mind. Instead, he let Jade walk ahead of him, just so he could watch her hips twitch as she moved.

"Precisely how far do I get to go with this *date* thing?" he asked in her ear.

"When I slug you, you'll know you've gone too far," she said without turning around.

"You're taking all the fun out of this."

"Yeah, 'cause that's what this is supposed to be—fun and games."

"You wouldn't be so crabby if you had some fun once in a while."

She halted. "Crabby?" she asked, turning to stare at him in amazement.

"If the mood fits…"

"Problem, J.B.?" Frank asked, his gaze darting between them.

Finally, Jade started moving again. "No. Let's just get this over with."

7

JADE STUCK CLOSE to her client as they wound their way through the crowded nightclub, music and partiers pulsing around them. So much for avoiding large groups of people.

And so much for her reestablishing distance.

His looks alone messed with her concentration. Darkly handsome in black pants and a gray, button-down shirt that matched his eyes and emphasized the breadth of his chest, Tremaine certainly turned heads as he passed. His proximity also brought its own kind of sweet torture. His hand in hers, his body brushing against her.

Added to her own personal hell were what seemed like eight thousand people who brushed by, bumped or just outright ran into them while they made their way to the second-floor meeting with Colin Hannigan.

She absolutely hated undercover work.

By the time they reached the table where the informant sat alone, she was more in the mood to shoot than pretend to flirt.

Hannigan looked a bit worse for wear than the most recent picture she'd found of him. His eyes were bloodshot and his clothes were wrinkled. He stood as they approached him. "You got an entourage now?" he asked, nervously eyeing Frank and David.

"New security team," Tremaine said with a shrug. "And my girlfriend, Mandy."

Jade jolted herself out of the shock of hearing how smoothly Tremaine had shifted into their cover story and managed to smile in what she hoped was a girlfriend-type way.

"Whoa, Mr. Smooth is off the market?"

"I'm afraid so. I hope you don't mind my bringing her. She's stuck to me like glue ever since the shooting."

Feeling like an idiot, but giving in to the part, Jade flipped her hair over her shoulder and gave Tremaine an affectionately annoyed look. "Especially since you seem to enjoy having dinner with overly skinny blondes when I'm not around."

"She was a business colleague, darling," he said.

"So you said."

Their mock disagreement had the effect they'd wanted—Hannigan relaxed. "No fighting, you two. We're celebrating." He extended his arm. "Have a seat."

Tremaine's eyebrows rose as he pulled out Jade's chair. "Celebrating?"

"Sure. You're here, aren't you? Failed hit and all that."

Though Jade had done a great many wild things in her career, the up-front, casual way Hannigan referred to a *hit* surprised even her.

Her client seemed to take the odd comment in stride. He chuckled as he slid into his chair. "Yeah, I'm still here, all right."

David and Frank took their positions on either side of the table silently, though with their earpieces they could hear every word she, Tremaine and Hannigan said, thanks to the monitoring device in the brooch on her dress and the one in Tremaine's watch.

The waitress took drink orders. Tremaine asked for a

whiskey, while Hannigan ordered a bottle of expensive champagne, which she was sure he had no intention of paying for.

They made inane small talk until she returned, and the
ceremony of cork-popping, pouring and toasting was complete. Jade was certainly no Miss Manners, but she still found
the whole business tacky. Then again, even Miss Manners
probably didn't have an etiquette policy for celebrating a
failed murder attempt.

"So, what's up?" Tremaine asked once the waitress left.

"There've been some rumbles about your shooting,"
Hannigan said.

Typically, Tremaine said nothing and waited for his informant to elaborate.

"There was a rumor a few weeks ago about a guy looking
for a hit man. No one came to me, but they asked a buddy of
mine. Said it was a high-profile deal with a local artist. My
buddy didn't have anything to do with it, but after you got
shot, it made me wonder."

"Who was the guy looking?"

"Some slickster from New York."

"How does he know that?"

"Guy gave him a business card with an NYC box
number on it."

"He give a description?"

"Dark."

Good grief, what an idiot. Jade looked around and pretended to sip her champagne.

"Dark as in African American, Mexican, Italian, what?"

"I think he meant dark, like dangerous."

"Interesting."

Hannigan polished off the rest of his champagne. Tremaine

had only taken a sip or two of his drink, while Hannigan had already downed a couple of glasses. Jade wasn't sure whether to encourage him to slow down or speed up. There was a fine line between loose and incoherent.

"Then," Hannigan went on, "last week another friend of mine said an art guy came around, asking questions about you."

"Art guy?"

"Peter Garner. You know him?"

Jade hoped only she could see the shocked, affirmative answer in Tremaine's expression.

"I've heard of him," he said.

"Anyway, this Garner guy had a card, too. Lots of people givin' out cards these days." Hannigan gave a what's-the-world-coming-to shake of his head. "He asks all these questions about you—what're you doin', where do you live and work, what're you like—personal stuff that's none of his business, you know?"

"And what did your friend tell him?"

"Nothin'. I mean, he doesn't know you. He only knows *I* know you. What could he say?"

Plenty. Like, give this Garner guy your name, address and phone number.

"A lot, Colin," Tremaine said. "Does your friend know you're meeting me tonight?"

Hannigan looked down, then shook his head.

He could be lying; he could just be nervous.

"Is he a good friend?" Tremaine asked.

"Sure. We hang out sometimes."

"So he knows where you live?"

"Yeah."

"Don't go back there. Frank?" When Frank appeared at Tremaine's side, he continued, "Can we put him somewhere?"

"We'll arrange it, Mr. Tremaine."

Hannigan paused with his glass halfway to his mouth. "Why—"

"You won't mind staying in a hotel suite for a few days in..."

"Clearwater, Florida," Frank finished.

"In Clearwater, will you?" As if he might actually need it, Tremaine added an encouraging smile.

"No, I guess not, but do you really think I need to hide?"

"I do."

"Did I do something wrong?"

"No. Given what happened to me, it's just a precaution."

"You think my buddy is okay?"

"I think he's fine. What's his name?" Tremaine asked.

"Johnny Malden."

"You can call him later if you like. Just don't tell him where you are."

Hannigan puffed out his chest. He was clearly enjoying his important role, even if he didn't realize the implications. "For security reasons, right?"

"Right."

Tremaine rose and Frank escorted Hannigan away from the table, though he looked longingly back at the half-full champagne bottle. Somebody would no doubt see to it that he had enough bubbles to make him forget about his lost buzz.

When Tremaine returned to his seat he said nothing, just stared into his nearly full whiskey glass.

"Peter Garner gets around," she said.

"Yes, he does. Let's dance."

"*Dance?*" She watched Frank disappear through the crowd with the informant. "We're not dancing. We're getting out of here."

He grabbed her hand and pulled her to her feet. "We'll get to that."

"This whole meeting is probably a setup. Hannigan could have been paid to lure you here."

"He wouldn't intentionally trap me."

"Don't tell me you trust him that much."

"I don't, but I would have known if he was lying. Let's go."

"I've got your back, boss," David put in, leaning toward them.

"I'm not worried about my back, I'm—" But Tremaine had already hustled her toward the stairs and, presumably, the dance floor. "Why are we doing this?"

"'Cause it's fun."

"That's open to interpretation."

Naturally, he didn't listen. She was in his arms on the dance floor, and though a rocking song played, and people gyrated around them, they glided together. "Peter Garner," she said in his ear.

"Surely you're not whispering another man's name in my ear."

"No, I'm shouting one. He's too close. How did he find out about Hannigan?"

He pulled her closer, his scent and heat enveloping her. "I don't know. Can we talk about it later?"

She wasn't crazy about it, but she let the point go. And though she knew she might regret her actions later, she laid her head against his chest. She absorbed his heartbeat, she felt his tension and need.

And she still wanted him.

Had she thought her feelings were going to subside? Had she thought she could focus solely on her job and not consider the attraction between them?

Even though she'd told him she could resist him, she'd known that was more wishful thinking than truth. She'd known all along their moment would arrive. She'd just hoped she could find the strength and commitment to put it off until she'd done her job, until he was safe.

Apparently, she wasn't as strong as she thought.

With Frank occupied in securing their informant and David needing to sleep off his shift, she had only Mo to get around to sneak her way into Tremaine's—well, hell, if she was contemplating sleeping with him she might as well refer to him by his first name—*Remy's* room.

And sneaking around Mo wasn't a walk in the park.

Not that she had a choice about being clandestine. She couldn't exactly be up-front and tell a member of her staff, *Oh, don't mind me, I'm just jumping into bed with our client.* Well, maybe she could. She just wouldn't be able to face them ever again.

Remy ran his hand down the back of her head, his fingers sliding through the strands of her hair. She closed her eyes and absorbed his touch. She longed to feel his body next to her, his warm, smooth skin gliding against her. She wanted him to fill the ache that pulsed through her every moment they were together. To forget all her responsibilities.

Sometimes she just wanted to be a woman again. An ordinary woman who worked, lived and loved.

But she wasn't ordinary, and neither was her job. Regrets got her nowhere, since she wouldn't give up her career to be normal. The missions and cases she'd completed—along with the skills she'd learned—defined her, surrounded her and saved her. She'd learned control and taken control of her life. Her job had given her power when she'd had none. It had been her companion and provided a focus in life, whereas before she'd simply been a victim.

That need for control had spilled over into everything else. She didn't trust people, and she certainly didn't let anyone close enough to her heart.

So, she didn't have a personal life.

Leaning on someone else, especially a man as lusciously tempting as Remington Tremaine, was a complete luxury. One she could indulge herself in for only a moment.

He had offered a wild, *temporary* affair.

"Stay with me tonight," he said into her ear as a slow song finally flowed from the overhead speakers.

She looked up at him. "Of course I'll—"

He laid his finger over her lips. "Don't you dare say anything about watching over or protecting me."

Since that's exactly what she'd been about to say, she pressed her lips together.

"Instead of sitting outside my door with a gun drawn, I'd prefer you slinking into my room in a pink—"

She frowned.

"No? Okay, a *blue,* mostly see-through bit of lingerie. Just as I drift off to sleep, you appear in the moonlight, then slip beneath the sheets and curl your body against mine."

Her heart hammered, but she shook her head. "I can't."

"You can. You *won't.*"

"We need to go."

"Back to the hotel? Where I lose you again to your job?"

She stepped back. "I was never off the job."

He jerked her against him. Even in the low light, she could see his eyes were glittering. Anger or desire? Maybe a combination of both. "This, us together, is *not* a job. You can fight what's between us, you can pretend it doesn't exist, but you won't dismiss it as part of a case."

She couldn't deny their attraction, but she'd hoped to put it off. Why did she suddenly feel as if she'd backpedaled so far she was against the wall?

Whatever this connection they had was, it was powerful. And even though she should be a professional and resist the allure, she knew now she wouldn't. Come hell or high water, as her mother would have said, she had to find out where her path with Remy led.

She nodded. "Understood."

She preceded him off the dance floor, where they joined David, and he radioed the driver to meet them at the back entrance of the club. By the time they entered the alley, though, the driver said he was caught in traffic. A wreck in front of the club had caused gridlock.

Jade sent David to spot the limo and help him find an alternate route, while she and Remy waited by the door. Given their mission, she didn't like the way her team was scattered, and that the car—their fastest means of escape—was trapped. But the club's kitchen door was behind them, she had a weapon and her client had skills that weren't even on the radar of her usual customers.

The night had cooled considerably, so she shivered as a breeze skimmed over her shoulders.

Remy laid his black leather jacket around her. "Where's your coat?"

"We went from the hotel to the limo, then into the club. I didn't bring a jacket." At his disappointed look, she added, "And I'm used to wearing more clothes than this. I didn't think about a coat."

"It's February. How do you not think about a coat?"

"I live in New Orleans. You never need a coat."

"Still—"

She held up her hand to stop him, then went still, listening to the night around them. The base from the club's sound system vibrated the ground. Dishes clanged in the kitchen. Horns and raised voices echoed from the streets.

Did she hear a crunch of gravel?

Another breeze whispered over her, fluttering the hair on her arms, sending chill bumps down the back of her neck.

Something wasn't right.

Remy felt it, too. He'd frozen. She barely sensed him breathing.

"Don't move," she whispered.

She shrugged out of Remy's jacket, then slid her feet out of her high-heeled sandals and wished like hell for her boots. She took two steps to her right, then sensed movement.

A man's arm swung toward her; a knife was clutched in his fist. Jade ducked, then swung, punching him in the stomach. She finished with a roundhouse kick to his head, dropping him to the ground immediately, his knife clattering on the pavement a few feet from his body.

Unsheathing her own knife, she planted her foot over his throat. "Don't even twitch," she said in a low, deadly tone.

He didn't. Probably because he could barely breathe.

Remy appeared beside her, his gun drawn. "Nice moves."

Still trying to catch her breath, Jade nodded, though she didn't take her gaze off their would-be assailant. "You wanna answer some questions?"

Red-faced, his eyes watering, the guy struggled to nod.

She eased up the pressure of her foot a little but kept her gaze on his. "You alone?"

He nodded.

"You got a problem with me?"

He shook his head.

She'd never seen the guy. He had brown hair, brown eyes and an ordinary face. The kind of guy you looked through or over—maybe to your detriment. Yet she didn't think he was a run-of-the-mill mugger. "You got a problem with him?" she asked, jerking her head back toward Remy.

Another shake.

"Who's paying you?"

The guy's eyes flashed for only a second, but distinctively enough that she had her answer. A paid attack.

"Why?"

Another shake.

He either didn't know or wasn't telling.

She should call the police. Or at least Detective Parker. She wanted to press her foot against his throat, to press her point and her questions. She had little doubt she'd get what she wanted. But she hesitated.

The prosecution of the attacker was being compromised every second she talked to him without the police or his attorney present.

"Allow me," Remy said, as if he sensed her struggle.

The intended victim questioning his attacker? No way.

"See if he's got ID," she said, hoping to give him a project that would prevent an argument.

Remy dug into the guy's back pocket and flipped open a worn brown wallet. "Johnny Malden."

"Surprise, surprise."

She pressed the panic button on her brooch that would bring her troops, then she dialed Detective Parker's cell. "You need to get to the back entrance of Club Pi. My client's been attacked again."

"How is he?"

"My client is fine. The attacker has been subdued."

"By whom?"

"The Easter bunny. Just get over here."

David ran to the scene as she disconnected. His gaze swept her, their client and the guy she had pinned to the ground. "You okay?"

"We're fine. Help me get him up."

As she stepped back and slid her feet into her impractical shoes, David and Remy dragged Malden to his feet. David secured his arms behind him with handcuffs.

They all stared silently at one another until the limo pulled around the corner and stopped next to them.

Their driver, Charlie, jumped out. "Sorry, boss. It's a damn mess out front."

"It's fine." The implications of the attempted attack were starting to zip through Jade's mind. Again, the whole thing was poorly planned, poorly executed. Was Peter Garner this sloppy or had he just hired somebody who was? And had gullible informant Colin Hannigan betrayed Remy on purpose or by accident?

A police cruiser and another car drove up a minute later. Detective Parker slid out of the unmarked car, while the officers hustled over to take charge of the suspect. After Jade exchanged David's cuffs for the cops' and handed over the wallet, Malden immediately requested his attorney. The thorough questioning Jade was sure the detective had been planning went straight out the window.

With little else to do, the officers tucked the suspect in the back of the patrol car and headed off.

"What happened, Ms. Broussard?" the detective asked, looking considerably more rumpled than when they'd seen him earlier.

Jade gave him a brief rundown of the attack.

"So he actually didn't assault your client. You assaulted him."

She crossed her arms over her chest. "He started it."

"You kicked him in those shoes?"

"I took them off."

He still looked as if he didn't believe she was the one who'd taken Malden down. Underestimation often worked in her favor.

"Did he say anything to you?" he asked.

"You mean did he voluntarily offer information to a witness of his criminal action?"

"Cute. Just answer the question."

"No."

Remy smiled, and Jade decided she'd definitely been hanging out with him too long, since she was enjoying telling the detective absolutely nothing.

"No, he didn't say anything? Nothing at all?"

"Nothing at all." Which he hadn't. He'd just given a few head shakes, and she'd discerned the rest. She really had nothing definitive to give Parker.

"How long ago did this incident occur?"

"Two minutes before I called you."

Behind his wire-rimmed glasses, he narrowed his eyes as if he didn't quite believe her, then his gaze slid over her and Remy. "You don't look much like a bodyguard tonight."

"No, I guess I don't."

The detective sighed. "Somehow I knew you were going to make this difficult. Were you at Club Pi tonight?"

"Yes."

"For what purpose were you there?"

This is where things got sticky. Revealing what she knew about Peter Garner could expose Remy's past to the police. The NSA's promise of no prosecution *might* hold.

But she wouldn't bet her client's life on it.

She already had off-duty cops watching Garner; involving yet another police department at this stage would complicate things. Not to mention, if the cops found out Hannigan was connected to Johnny Malden, they'd want to talk to him. Given the fact that they'd hustled him out of town, that was going to be difficult.

If there was ever a trial, she'd be sure Hannigan appeared with a cooperative smile. For now, though, she had to skate the truth.

"My client met a friend for drinks."

"What friend?"

"Mr. Colin Hannigan. I believe he's a resident of Atlanta." Remy added a nod.

The detective looked around. "Where's this friend now?"

"He left."

"And went where?"

"The last time I saw him, he was walking down the stairs. I didn't ask where he was going."

Obviously deciding he'd had enough of her evasive answers, he turned to Remy. "Whose idea was it to meet for drinks at Club Pi?"

"Mr. Hannigan's."

Parker smiled. "Ah, we're finally getting somewhere. Do you suspect Mr. Hannigan of hiring—" he flipped open the wallet "—Johnny Malden to attack you?"

"No."

Parker looked exasperated. "No?"

He was asking the right questions, but he wasn't making a complete connection. Jade felt sorry for him. Not doing everything she could to help the police was difficult for her. She'd been raised to support and respect cops. But she didn't know this one well, and she didn't want to bring anybody into their circle and expose Remy's past.

Was protecting a thief any more morally compromising than protecting a politician?

"Do you know Mr. Malden?" he finally asked.

"No."

The detective settled his hands at his waist. "You people are just plain nuts."

"Hannigan and Malden aren't important," Jade said.

"The D.A. isn't likely to agree with you." He pointed at himself. "*I* don't agree with you."

"Who they're connected to is what's important. Somebody is hiring people to go after my client."

"How do you know that? Malden didn't say anything, and we have no leads on the shooter."

"Instinct."

Parker held her gaze for a moment or two, then he shook his head. He seemed like a pretty decent cop, so he had to suspect there was a whole lot she wasn't telling him, but he must also sense he'd never get her to talk. "Fine. I need all of you to come to the station to—"

"Mr. Tremaine and I were the only witnesses."

"Whatever. I still need you to come down to the station and give your official statements."

Jade cast a glance at Remy, then David. She wasn't crazy about that idea, but neither did she want Parker to know their location. He may realize Remy hadn't been home if they'd been watching his apartment, but that was as much as she was willing to give him. And she still needed to pick up the copy of the case file Frank had gotten for them.

"It's a police station," Parker said at her hesitation. "We're the good guys, remember?"

"It's not you I'm worried about, it's your customers."

"You are one paranoid lady."

"That's what they pay me for."

"And one with influence. You got that case file pretty quickly."

She said nothing. This conversation was going down a path she didn't need Parker exploring. "Let's go, Charlie," she said, still facing Parker. For him, she forced a smile. "Thank you for your quick response. We'll be down in the morning to give our statements."

Turning, she led Remy to the limo. David got in and closed the door behind them, and they'd pulled away before the detective even moved.

"What is he going to find out about Hannigan?" she asked Remy. His friend and sometime informant was the weakest link to their story.

"Nothing. Colin is a federal government informant. The local cops won't know anything about him except his rap sheet. He'd consider it beneath him to help them."

"Beneath him? No wonder the police can't solve crimes these days."

"Even criminals have standards."

Oh, good grief.

8

AT THE HOTEL, with a diet soda in her hand, Jade paced in front of her client and her team. Even Mo, who'd been relaxing and watching a pay-per-view movie in the other room, had joined the discussion of the attempted assault. Only Frank was absent, as he was stowing Hannigan at a beach hotel and wouldn't make it back until morning.

"Again, a poorly planned attack, with way too many unpredictable barriers. How did the attacker know we'd come out the back? He *guessed?* And there was no way to foresee the traffic jam the limo got caught in. Plus, if Frank hadn't taken Hannigan off and I hadn't sent David to check on the limo, there would have been four of us."

"Maybe he intended to distract the others by holding you hostage, then go for Tremaine," Mo said.

"How could he have known I'd be there?"

"Maybe he thought I'd be alone," Remy said.

"That's more likely. Hannigan could have told Malden more about you than he thought. Maybe he and Garner figured you'd come alone."

"From our research into Garner, he seems pretty slick," David said. "Would he really hire somebody as clumsy as Malden?"

"I would think he'd be smoother," Remy said.

"Could be trying to throw us off by being sloppy," Mo said.

"Maybe, but after calling Remy to offer money for the ring, he'd pretty much blown any chance of flying under his radar."

"None of this makes sense," Remy said as he stood. He walked over to the windows, turned his back to them and slid his hands in the pockets of his tailored pants.

The solitary pose affected Jade as much as it had earlier, when he'd talked about the murder of his D.A. friend. She wanted to walk up behind him, slide her arms around him and send some of her heat into his body. She wanted to remind him he wasn't alone anymore.

Oh, yeah, Miss Bodyguard? And is that just a professional assurance?

"These attacks just don't seem like him," he said. "Peter is very intelligent and cultured. He's a premier authenticator of historical and contemporary art. He's not sloppy, and he doesn't take unnecessary risks."

"Something seems to have changed," she said.

"Maybe he's desperate," David said.

"For a fifty-dollar ring," she added. A ring that was obviously a key to something else. Was it possible it had some historical value—like the gun that killed Lincoln? "Mo, why don't you make contact with our surveillance teams? Let's find out what our suspect has been up to tonight."

As Mo rose from the sofa and headed to the computer equipment, David turned to Remy. "Ah, Mr. Tremaine—"

"Remy, please."

David looked to Jade. She normally insisted that her staff address their clients formally to maintain professional objectivity. But nothing about this case was normal, so she nodded.

"Remy, are you sure about this Hannigan guy? You said he

was a gambler. Maybe he got himself into trouble, and Garner offered him enough money to get out."

"It's possible, but if he needed money, he'd be more likely to come to me to get it."

"I'm not sure it matters either way," Jade said. "He's tucked away where he can't do any more damage—intentional or not."

"Good point," David said.

"Why don't you guys start your sleep shifts? We're bound to have fresh ideas in the morning."

David got to his feet and waved as he headed to the other room. It had been a long day, and he was no doubt glad to see it end. Remy, however, still stood by the window, his hands tucked in his pants pockets.

"You, too," she said to him.

"Are you going to bed?"

"Yes."

He walked toward her, stopping just before their bodies brushed. "With me?" he whispered.

Oh, boy. She swallowed. And stalled. "I need to shower, then we'll…talk."

He brushed a strand of hair off her face. "I'll be waiting."

"WHAT THE HELL am I doing?"

Remy was lying flat on his back, in the dark, waiting for a woman who'd most likely never come.

This need for her wasn't normal. This idea that they were connected in some destined, elemental way was ridiculous. And seeking her out at the precise moment his life splashed into the toilet seemed even less sane.

The fact that her professional attitude about her job was holding her back—the very thing saving his ass—was almost funny. If he didn't have such a serious case of uncontrollable lust, he might laugh.

But nothing about the past few days was laughable.

Peter Garner.

Given recent events, his suspicions about Garner murdering Sean Nagel seemed accurate. As Remy had many times, he considered simply telling the NSA Garner was connected to a smuggling case—not a stretch—then launch an official investigation that would set him up, and make sure he didn't escape with his life.

Simple. Direct. Over.

Remy slid his hand into his pocket and pulled out the onyx signet ring. He'd carried it with him for the last four months.

Why had he lied to Jade?

Habit? No, he could admit he didn't trust her fully. He trusted her with his life and to do what was in his best interest, but he also knew she'd do the right thing. And when it came to Garner, *right* wasn't necessarily his choice. He needed more flexibility to respond to whatever Garner tossed his way.

Mostly right would more accurately describe his approach. Which was certainly better than mostly wrong—the way he'd lived his life for many years.

Sister Mary Katherine had convinced him he wouldn't go to hell for his sins as long as he repented. Would God buy *mostly* repented? Then again, maybe He'd decided hell on earth would be a more fitting punishment, so He'd sent Remy a bodyguard with a killer body, luscious lips and a laserbeam gaze that made his heart jump and his groin swell.

Would she hate him if he took his vengeance on Garner? Or—given that she'd done the same thing in avenging her parents—would she be the one person who'd understand?

But he couldn't kill Garner too soon or else the secrets would die with him. Could Remy move his life forward before finally learning the ring's significance?

He reached down to his ankle holster and unstrapped it, setting his revolver on the nightstand beside him. He pulled out the lock pick set tucked within the holster and used a pick to pop the stone out of the ring. Underneath was a single, jagged piece of metal, which appeared to be the prong holding the stone, though he'd always imagined it was some sort of a key. It had a pattern of grooves too deliberate to be random, and the metal was thick and strong.

But a key to what?

He startled at a sound from the living room and shoved the ring back in his pocket a second before Jade rushed into the room.

She was breathing hard as she leaned back against the door. She'd changed out of her dress and put on jeans and a black T-shirt. "I didn't come in here to talk to you."

Heart hammering, he sat up. "You didn't? Is everything okay?"

She shook her head, then nodded. "I told Mo I needed to talk to you."

"But you don't?"

"No."

"What do you need?"

She walked toward him, then slid her hand around the back of his head, her fingers stroking his hair. "You. Just you."

He braced his hands at her waist. He wanted to yank her into his lap and devour her, yet he also wanted to savor the moment. His erection pulsed. His blood warmed in anticipation.

Her eyes darkened with smoky need as she leaned forward,

her body pressed against his, pushing him onto his back. "I don't get involved in relationships, remember? But I need you. I don't know what you did, or even how you did it, but I can't let it go.

"You've captured me in a way I didn't think I could be. I can't fight it anymore. I don't want to," she added in a whisper.

He cupped her cheek with his hand and pulled her head toward his. Her breath brushed his face. Tenderness washed over him, followed quickly by excitement, expectation.

The moment their mouths met, the heat exploded. Her tongue pushed past his lips, sliding against his. His skin caught fire. Her body pulsed and warmed beneath his hands.

He gripped her waist, molding her hips to his. The pressure was pleasure and pain. He moaned.

"Quietly," she said against his lips.

"You've *got* to be kidding."

He didn't want Mo charging in here, but he wasn't sure he was capable of restraint. He wanted her naked. A moan on her part wouldn't be unwelcome.

Pulling her head back to his, he kissed her hard, then yanked her T-shirt from her jeans. He ran his hands underneath the soft cotton, over her stomach and cupped her breasts in his palms. With a flick of his thumbs, he slid them beneath her bra. Her nipples hardened at his touch, and she let a soft sigh escape against his mouth.

"Better," he whispered. "Much better."

But he wanted more. Skin to skin. Heartbeat to heartbeat.

He flipped her over and straddled her, then pulled off her T-shirt. The soft, needy look on her face made him smile, made him want to do whatever it took to keep the expression there. He reached behind her and unhooked her bra, tossed it aside, then trailed his tongue across her skin. She tasted sweet, better than he'd ever imagined.

She arched her back, straining toward him, silently asking for more. He sucked her nipple into his mouth, his tongue laving the exquisite contrast of hard and soft. In his periphery he could see her other nipple silently begging for equal attention. After bestowing the same, hungry treatment on it, he kissed a trail up to her neck. He inhaled her clean scent and paused a moment to revel in the simple closeness of their bodies. In all of his fantasies he had never dreamed that she would feel so good, that her skin would caress his with such an erotic flair.

His heart hammered against his chest. His erection pressed against the fly of his pants demanding satisfaction.

He could hold her later—he'd have to. Now, he couldn't wait to be inside her.

She obviously had the same idea, as she started unbuckling his belt, then unbuttoning and unzipping his pants. She cupped him confidently in her hand, and he let his head drop back, sucking in a breath as he made a desperate grab for control of his body. The firm stroke of her fingers was nearly too much.

"Condoms?" she whispered.

"In my bag," he managed to say.

"Oh, right."

She let go of him and scooted off the bed, returning a moment later with several foil packets. She stripped off her jeans while he tossed off his clothes and rolled on the protection just as quickly.

They met again on the bed, kneeling to face each other—completely bare this time. Completely open to each other.

No, not yet. As much as he'd anticipated this moment,

there were too many issues still between them for that kind of honesty. Soon, maybe, he'd be completely open with her, share all that he'd kept hidden. But at this moment the only thing he could focus on was the tempting woman in his arms.

He kissed her, a slow, deep, sensual meeting of their mouths that spiked the tension between them. He ran his hands over her sexy body from her thighs to the sides of her breasts and back again. As she pressed closer he grasped the back of her knees, lifting them and urging her back onto the bed with the weight of his upper body. After wrapping her legs around his waist, he braced himself on his forearms. The heat of her sex against his erection sent a wave of lust through him that was so powerful he had to grit his teeth against the urge to bury himself deep inside her.

Meeting her gaze, he brushed her hair off her face and nudged the entrance to her body. "You're so beautiful."

She shook her head.

"You are," he said. "And for once, I'm in charge, so I have the final say." She lifted her hips, a move that pushed the sensitive tip of his erection just inside her. He sucked in a breath. "Then again, maybe not."

No longer able to resist, he thrust his hips forward and surged into her, feeling a hot rush of satisfaction and pure hunger shoot through his body. Her fingers gripped his back and she let out a low moan. Fearing interference from her team and a premature end to their private time, he covered her mouth with his.

She tightened her legs around him, bringing him in deeper with each of his thrusts. Beads of sweat popped out on his skin. His breathing grew labored. He wanted to hold out, to prolong the pleasure, but his control was weakening. She felt so amazingly tight and wet. She threw her whole body into moving against him, and he felt the effects all the way down to his toes.

As his orgasm approached, he tore his mouth from hers and prayed she was growing closer, as well. He needed her with him when he came. He cupped her backside and changed the angle of her body. She closed her eyes and increased her pace.

She was close. Very close.

Yes.

His body was roaring to completion, his breath forced out in quick pants. As he felt her squeeze his erection like a fist, his orgasm consumed him, pulsing in time with hers. He bucked and desperately tried to suck in air, finally collapsing on top of her like a fish denied water.

Her heart thumped erratically beneath his ear. Her body was completely relaxed, a position he doubted she assumed very often.

"Talk about crossing the line," she said quietly, though she slid her fingers through his hair as if letting him know she didn't blame him.

"But it was worth it."

She continued sliding her hands back and forth in an absent caress. "Yeah, it was."

"Will you stay with me a while?"

"I'm not inclined to move, so I guess I will."

"You could enjoy it."

"I'll probably do that, too."

He managed to dredge up enough strength to roll off her and to his side. He propped his head in his hand, trailing his fingers down her bare, damp skin. She was flushed and

relaxed. He decided he liked that just as much as command-
ing and fierce.

"We're good together."

Her gaze flicked to his and held. "Like this, yes."

"Not in other ways?"

"I don't think so."

He frowned. He wanted to argue with her, tell her whatever
problems they had could be worked out even though they
were different people with opposite outlooks on life. Despite
the complications and their issues of trust and acceptance,
there was a part of him that wanted to let their chemistry
sweep it all away. How like Jade to be honest—even in bed,
where lying was prevalent way too often between couples.
"We could be."

She stiffened. "A wild, temporary affair—that's what we
agreed to."

"You have my signature on this?"

"Do I need it?"

Why was he arguing the point? An affair suited him as well
as it did her. Neither of them had the time or patience for a
relationship. He should be concentrating on getting his life
back, focusing on the moment and not thinking about what
possibilities lay beyond the end of this case.

"No," he said finally. "Affair agreed. But no holding back."

"And we tell my staff nothing."

"They're bound to notice you sleeping in my room every
night."

"No, they won't, because I won't be doing that."

"I won't lie to them. I won't pretend our relationship is just
professional."

She sat up. "Remy—"

He pulled her on top of him, though he hated to interrupt his name falling from her lips. Maybe because she'd denied him that pleasure for so long. "I can't pretend one thing and live another."

Her jaw dropped. "That's what you do every day."

"Not with us." He slid his thumb across her bottom lip. "Something about my life has to be real. Do you know how long it's been since I shared a conversation with someone— at least someone not wearing a religious habit—about my life, my *real* life? Do you know how hard it is to keep so much inside, to lie and deceive everyone you know and meet?"

"I do."

"I don't know why this is happening to me, now, with you. But I know I want more. I want to be honest, and I want to talk to someone who understands, someone who's been there. Someone I admire."

She bowed her head briefly, then surprised him by laying her head against his bare chest. "I share my work with Frank, but I share myself with nobody. For as long as we're together, for as long as the case lasts, I won't hold back. But I think the odds are good that we'll spend a lot of time arguing."

Probably. He kissed her temple. "We might surprise each other."

"Maybe." She lifted her head. "Are we allowed to talk about the case?"

He smiled and stroked her jaw. For such a tough woman, her skin was amazingly soft. "You're allowed to do anything you want."

She wriggled off him and left the bed. "Then I need to get dressed."

He reached out and grabbed her hand. "Then no case."

"I can't talk to you naked."

Standing, he cupped her bare backside, molding her hips against his already hardening groin. "If you insist."

She pulled away from him. "See, this is why I have to have clothes on to talk to you."

Sighing about the inevitable, he picked up his shirt from the floor. He tossed it to her as he walked into the bathroom to get himself a towel. "I'll give this fifteen minutes."

"It's *your* case we need to talk about, you know," she called after him.

After splashing cold water on his face—and other parts— he returned with the towel slung around his waist. "I'm aware of that."

Still buttoning Remy's shirt over her chest, Jade didn't look up at his words. She was too busy inhaling his spicy scent still clinging to the fabric, and marveling over the silky texture. The sensual effect he had permeated every part of her. Her body still vibrated from his touch. Her skin felt hot. Her pulse raced.

She wanted him again. In a variety of positions and many times over.

"I just need to—" She finally looked up, and her breath froze in her throat.

He stood several yards away, the bathroom light outlining his broad-shouldered frame. Beads of either water or sweat rolled down his tanned skin. His washboard abs rippled above the white towel hanging low on his hips. His dark hair was pushed off his face, and his sliver eyes glowed.

He was a fantasy. He'd stepped out of a dream she'd had at some point in her life when she'd still believed dreams came true. When she'd thought she'd be whole and loved again.

When had she stopped dreaming? When had cynicism set in? When had she started countering tenderness with sarcasm?

He forced her to remember she wasn't just a security expert, bodyguard, marksman or former agent. She was a woman with hopes and dreams and needs. She wanted so much more for herself than just her job. But that first step into real intimacy was a doozie.

And though she'd compromised her professionalism— something she'd sworn she would never do again—she sensed he might be worth it. Was it possible he could give her all she needed and more?

"What?" he asked, holding out his arms.

Knees weak, she sank onto the bed. "Nothing." She shook her head in an effort to clear her thoughts. "I just—I had *something* to say."

He walked toward her and gripped her elbows. "You were amazing tonight at the club."

Her gaze dipped briefly to his nearly bare body. *Dear heaven, the man is blessed. And not in a way Sister Mary Katherine would know about.* "You think so?" she managed to say, though without her usual hardiness.

"You had that guy pinned to the ground before I'd even thought to move."

"Mmm, well, I saw him first."

"I doubt it would have mattered."

"Not upset that a woman defended you?"

"Hell, no." He angled his head, his gorgeous face partly shadowed in the low light, giving him a dark, mysterious appearance. "Not that I'm sending out a group e-mail announcement about it."

She curled her lip.

He trailed his finger along her bare thigh, sending waves of heat through her body. "I'd rather demonstrate my appreciation in other, more *personal* ways."

"Keep it up, and next time I'll send the kick in your direction."

He gripped the collar of her—actually his—shirt, then pulled it away from her neck so he could place soft, lingering kisses beneath her ear. "Have I told you that you look very sexy wearing my shirt?"

Her breath was clogging her throat, and she fought to hold on to some semblance of sanity. "You just did."

He flicked his tongue over her earlobe. "Maybe I should emphasize my point."

She gasped. "You just did."

His lips slid to her jaw. "I'm pretty sure I need to go further."

Before she remembered to argue, he'd unbuttoned the shirt. His warm, confident hands cupped her breasts, and she let her head fall back as she absorbed his touch. When was the last time she'd wanted a man's hands on her so much? When had she been unable to talk about a case or keep her focus?

Ah…never.

Her nipples hardened as his thumbs caressed them into aching peaks. She went damp between her legs. The desire always shimmering beneath the surface roared into focus again.

"I need you," he whispered against her throat. "I need you constantly."

He trailed his hand down her stomach, then slid his fingers into the warmth of her sex. She gasped as relief, pleasure and a craving for more all shot down her spine.

"Quietly," he said, obviously enjoying her torture.

He pushed his finger up and down slowly, then faster, then slow again. Her breathing accelerated. The hunger intensified.

"How about *quickly?*"

He complied for a second or two. "Like this?"

She gripped his shoulders to keep from collapsing at his feet. "Oh…ah, yes."

Just as she could feel her desire spiraling upward, striving toward a peak, he slowed again.

She nearly cried. "You're killing me."

"Yeah? This is what it's like for me every minute of the day. When you come close to me or smile at me, I soar. When you look like you'd rather punch me, when I feel your disappointment, I drop."

Wasn't it the same for her? She couldn't explain it, and wasn't sure she liked it, but her emotions and reactions were tied up with his. Her world had become centered around him so quickly, so surely. She was scared and exhilarated at the same time.

"I'm at your mercy now, though," she said, knowing she needed to try to give him the words and truth he gave her.

"Yes, you are."

As he continued placing silky kisses along her neck and shoulders, and his finger prolonged its erratic rhythm, she knew she was going to faint or explode. She rolled her hips forward in an effort to deepen his touch, her body straining for completion.

"This what you need?" he asked as he slid two fingers inside her.

Oh, yes.

She couldn't speak. She just clung to him. She never let anyone control her, yet here she was, in the middle of a dangerous, critical case, and she was letting a man, a *client* she'd known barely twenty-four hours, play her like a stringed instrument.

More remarkably, she wanted more. She wanted to deepen their connection, she wanted to know him better, to share her concerns, to understand the way he thought.

Her muscles tightened around his fingers. Her legs trembled.

Then the bottom fell out. Her orgasm pulsed through her body with the force of a series of kicks, wringing every last drop of need and energy from her.

By the time she'd returned to earth and opened her eyes, she realized he still stood in front of her, the towel wrapped around his waist. He was smiling.

He hadn't— Didn't he want to—

"What about you?" she managed to ask.

"Watching you was enough." He cupped her cheek. "For the moment."

9

FEELING A BIT FOOLISH that she'd gotten so carried away, Jade gathered the edges of her shirt together. "I should go."

"I thought you wanted to discuss the case."

What case? she almost asked.

He'd rattled her way too much. Wasn't it enough she'd completely compromised her professionalism? Did she have to further humiliate herself by forgetting she even *had* a job?

On the edge of being orgasmic, she had optimism. Back to reality, regret and uncertainty took over.

"We can talk tomorrow," she said, searching the room for her clothes.

He wrapped his fingers around her wrist and held her in place. "Don't go."

She closed her eyes. Her pulse beat hard and strong where he touched her. So many emotions raced around inside her, she couldn't keep track of them all. "I'm embarrassing myself."

"You're not. You couldn't with me."

She'd let down her guard and now she couldn't figure out how to reconstruct the walls.

He gathered her clothes and boots, then handed them to her. Nodding toward the bathroom, he said, "Get dressed. I'll wait for you out here."

She latched on to the chance to escape without a backward

glance. She didn't look at herself in the mirror as she tossed on her clothes and splashed water on her face. She never avoided confrontation. Hell, confrontation was part of her job.

Turning away from the lurking mirror, she shoved her feet into her boots and felt almost normal. She wished she had her pistol, but it was lying on her bedside table in the other room.

Be ready for anything, at any time, Frank had once said to her. *If that means sleeping with your gun at your side, or not sleeping at all, then that's what you do.*

At the moment, she didn't much feel like the student Frank had believed held so much promise. She didn't feel like the righteous avenger she'd been at nineteen. She didn't even feel like the kick-ass agent she'd become over time.

She felt guilty.

And, for the first time in a very long time, fear rolled over her. Remy's life was on the line. This man she cared about and shared an intimacy with she couldn't even begin to explain was in grave danger. The lines between client and lover blurred, causing everything else to blur. She couldn't be scared and do her job. She had to focus.

Turning, she finally faced herself.

She saw an average-looking woman with rumpled hair and clothes. Her makeup had been kissed or worn off, making her skin paler and her freckles stand out. But the intensity in her eyes cheered her, even with the shadows beneath them. She was ready to fight again.

As she stalked into the bedroom, she noticed Remy had changed into jeans and a plain white T-shirt. She'd always seen him dressed elegantly, so the change made her stomach jump.

She forced herself to sit on the edge of the bed beside him. She forced herself to think.

"Where do you think the ring came from?"

"I think it was part of a business deal or heist that Garner and Nagel pulled off. Or, more likely, Garner hired Nagel to commit."

"Thieves stick together."

His eyes were blank as he looked over at her. "Like me?"

"But you're not. Not anymore."

"Are you so sure?"

Was he messing with her? Did he enjoy challenging her? *Oh, yeah. A big, fat yes.*

But maybe he was really hurt by her distaste for his former life. Well, she didn't see how that could change. No matter how he'd managed to justify it to himself, he'd taken from others and profited. That was just…wrong.

Not that she hadn't made mistakes in her life. Some people would probably say the people she'd killed—even in the name of justice and by direction of her government—were victims. Many more would adversely judge her for taking revenge on her parents' killer. Was she so pure? Was *anybody?*

"I can hear your moralistic wheels turning, you know," he said, linking hands with her.

She glanced down at their joined fingers and wished she could feel uncomfortable with the contact.

"The ring was probably part of the take," he said.

"But it's not worth much."

"I've often wondered if it's a key to finding something else. Like a clue to where a treasure is buried."

"Sounds a bit far-fetched. And if Nagel was such a great family friend, why didn't he tell you why he wanted it? It seems to me, he wanted to trick a young boy out of something he knew was valuable."

"Could be. Regardless, he died with that secret."

"So, how did it wind up in your possession?"

"Since Garner wound up killing Nagel, I wonder if Nagel had stolen the ring, betrayed him in some way."

"Still, how did it get from Nagel to your mother to you?"

He shrugged, and goose bumps prickled her skin. He was holding back—again. He knew, or suspected, where the ring had come from.

Why did he continually refuse to give her the information she needed to solve *his* case? Why wouldn't he trust her?

He'll never trust anybody. He's a thief.

A point she always needed to keep in mind. And regardless of his suspicions or his motives, he certainly knew where the ring was now.

She rose, letting go of his hand, and stared down at him. "I need to see the ring."

He stood and picked his pants up off the floor. Reaching into the pocket, he pulled out an object he dropped in her palm.

It was a worn-looking ring in a silver setting with a scratched onyx stone.

Anger bubbled in her veins. "You had it all the time."

"Yes."

She curled her fingers around the ring. "You lied."

He nodded, and she felt an answering wrench of pain near her heart. "I did."

"Why?"

"It's not about us. I just—"

"I get it." She fisted her hands at her sides, her body throbbing with fury. "You didn't lie to me, your lover, just me, your security chief." Glaring up at him, she jutted her chin forward. "Did you notice we're the same person?"

He reached for her. "Jade, I—"

She took a big step backward, both mentally and physically. She couldn't believe she'd trusted this man, this *thief,* to actually be up front with her.

He wanted to save his own ass, of course, but he didn't want to cooperate or listen to advice. And his own agenda bubbled beneath the surface all the time. For all she knew, he'd killed Nagel and taken the ring. Using a nun as an alibi would be part of the kick. "This is exactly why I didn't want to get involved. Separate business from pleasure? Who does that?" She rocked back on her heels. "But let's ridiculously assume you can separate me from my job. Any particular reason you felt the need to lie to the person in charge of your security?"

"I didn't fully trust you."

"No kidding?" She turned away, not wanting him to see how much that hurt. "That's probably wise in retrospect since I may shoot you myself and get this whole, beyond-annoying case over with."

"Please look at me."

"No."

She sensed him moving behind her. He laid his hands on her shoulders. "I should have trusted you."

God, she wanted to hit him. *"You think?"*

"I'm sorry I didn't. I don't trust anybody. I never have."

"Except Sister Mary Katherine." She glared at him over her shoulder. "Or is that a lie, too?"

His eyes were bleak. "It's not. You know it's not."

True, she'd checked out his background, but she had only his word about his bond with the nun. She had only his version of the investigation concerning the ring. She had only his suspicions that a respected art dealer was actually a murderer.

Did she understand his struggle with trusting anybody?

Yes.

Did she think of him and Garner in the same category?

No.

She didn't believe Remy capable of killing in cold blood. Not even for a big profit. Even through her anger, she knew the thrill of evading security, of being somewhere he wasn't supposed to be, of beating the system, of possessing something he shouldn't have, was the kick for him. The money was just a side benefit.

He had the nerve to give her his half grin. "You're going to forgive me."

She turned to face him, crossing her arms over her chest. "Maybe, but I'm still pissed, so keep your distance." Calmer, she examined the ring clutched in her fist. "Not that I doubted you, but you're right, the jewelry itself isn't the valuable part."

"Definitely not."

The trinket in her hand had cost one man his life and was threatening her client's. There had to be more than she saw. "So let's go with your earlier theory. Is the ring *part* of the heist or part of the solution to finding something else?"

"Like more treasure? What do you think?"

She examined the ring from every side. Crossing to the lamp at the bedside, she flipped it on and looked at the ring under the bright light. "Have you ever popped out the stone? Maybe there's a secret message concealed inside."

"Like a fortune cookie?"

"Sure." This case only got more bizarre by the second. "Why not?"

He moved toward her, taking the ring from her hands and using a metal, toothpick-size gadget to pop the stone from the setting. The gadget disappeared back into his pocket. "Is that a lock pick?" she asked.

"Yes."

"The one you used to break into my room last night?"

"Yes."

"You know, Tremaine, you can be very trying to a woman's patience."

He leaned close, his heat washing over her. "The next time you're on the verge of an orgasm, I'm going to make you call me Tremaine before I send you over."

Her throat went dry. "Are you threatening me?"

His eyes sparked with challenge. "I'm promising you."

"You're certainly arrogant, assuming you'll even get me in such a vulnerable position again."

"I'll get you there, all right." He smiled and drew his index finger from her chin to the spot just between her breasts. "You want me to prove it?"

She vividly recalled his body moving in and out of hers, the need that crawled over her skin every time he was near her. She cleared her throat. "I've got things to do, just now. Maybe later."

She didn't like his confident smirk, but she was distracted by the ring—minus its stone—that she held in her hand. "What the hell is that?" she asked, staring at the jagged metal prong, which looked amazingly like a key.

"What do you think?"

"It looks like a key."

"I think so, too."

"To what?"

"I have no idea, but I think we may be about to find out." He ran his finger down the edge of the mini key. "Any guesses what it unlocks?"

"A bus station locker? A handcuff? Hell, it's small enough to fit a mini padlock on a preteen girl's diary."

"The possibilities are endless."

"Which is why you haven't learned its significance before now."

"Is that a compliment?"

She cut her gaze toward him. "I'm still pissed at you, but yes. The big question seems to be, why now? If Garner killed Nagel all those years ago, why is he just coming after the ring now?"

"Even more troubling is the idea that I've had the ring all my life—my mother left it, and me, with the nuns when I was six months old. Why does Nagel wait fifteen years to seek it—and me—out? Then Garner waits another twenty to do the same thing?"

"We have a lot more investigating to do."

He slid his arms around her. "You're not dumping me after I lied?"

"No, I guess not." Her heart was already hammering at his touch. She had about as much choice in seeing this through to the end as she did taking her next breath. What started as a case had become a quest.

She knew better than anybody that the past was capable of defining the future, and until Remy knew the truth about his past, he couldn't move on. Her job was to help him find that peace—or at least bring about a conclusion.

The only difference was that her mission had become personal.

He pulled her tight against his chest and kissed her forehead. "There's something else I haven't told you."

She breathed in his sexy heat and tried to remember why that was important. "No kidding?"

"Nagel might have been my father."

"YOUR FATHER?" Jade echoed, her tone hollow.

Remy had definitely screwed up by holding back on her. He'd known it the moment he'd lied, but holding back was so natural to him it seemed part of his DNA. He'd told nobody of the ring's significance, yet there were people now after him for it. Even after thirty-five years, the cheap thing fascinated anyone who came into contact with it.

It held the key to his past. And his future.

"That's what he told me when he came to see me at the orphanage."

"He was your father, he'd given you the ring at your birth and now he wanted it back?"

"Yes."

"And for the previous fifteen years he'd been…?"

"Scrambling. Though he didn't say that at the time. I learned later about his connection to Garner, some Mob people and your basic seedy underworld." His legacy. Wasn't it beautiful? "Can you handle sleeping with a second-generation criminal?" he asked quietly.

She met his gaze, her eyes soft with understanding. "You're not responsible for him."

"Just for my own actions. Which aren't too pretty, either."

"He *abandoned* you and your mother. You'd never do that."

An amazing kind of relief rippled through him. "No, I wouldn't."

"Let me pace." She slid out of his arms, and he knew she wasn't rejecting him, just falling into her usual mode of thinking. "You said he *might* have been your father. You're not sure?"

"I only have his word."

"But you've been trying to find his murderer ever since."

"Because he might be."

"It's damn noble, you know."

He shook his head. "I'm a lot of things, Jade. Noble isn't one of them."

She stopped and smiled at him. "You're not a bad guy, Tremaine, you're just trying to be."

Warmth spread through his body, even as he tried to deny her belief in him. Wouldn't he just disappoint her later?

"Your mother omitted your father's name from your birth certificate to protect you," she added.

He'd waffled between hoping so and cursing her decision. "It's possible."

She laid her palm against his chest. "Your mother couldn't stand the idea of you being brought up in such a dangerous environment. Sister Mary Katherine was obviously right about him being a hoodlum." Her gaze searched his. "Garner knows your father's identity."

He'd thought the same thing. "Maybe. If Nagel is my father, did he tell Garner he'd given the ring to his son for safe keeping? Did Garner demand he get it back?"

"Or was your father someone else entirely? Someone not involved with either of them? Maybe he really did own the ring from the beginning, and Nagel and Garner conspired to get it from him, and—ultimately—you."

"Could be." He nodded at the ring and its odd key. "And that's how we find out."

She handed the ring back to him, then massaged her forehead. "My brain is fuzzy. I need to think. I need sleep." She walked around him and headed toward the door. "Alone."

A sense of panic, a need to hold her, invaded him. "I'd rather you stay."

She reached for the doorknob and kept her back to him. "I can't."

"I am sorry for lying to you. It won't happen again."

"I believe you."

"Sort of, anyway."

"Sort of." She glanced back at him. "I'll get him for you."

"Let's get him together."

REMY LAID AWAKE long into the night thinking about pasts and mistakes, about futures and promises. Maybe that was natural for a man whose life was on the line—even more so than it usually was.

When he finally fell asleep, he dreamed of his mother, with her long, dark hair and warm, brown eyes. She sang to him in a soft voice, wearing a flowing, Bohemian skirt and lighting candles that smelled like tangy ocean water. She was beautiful and comforting. He longed for her to hold him.

Then her face changed.

It became paler, with freckles, and Jade's voice came out of her mouth. *I'm at the end of my patience with you.* Her eyes turned bright green and softened with tenderness and desire. *You've captured me in a way I didn't think I could be.* Her eyes narrowed; her body tensed. *Or is that a lie, too?*

He was completely wrapped up in her. He wanted her time and attention. He was fascinated by her face, her moods and her strength. He needed her expertise.

Though he'd settle for her body.

With that thought, he woke as he usually did. Suddenly, with an immediate awareness of his surroundings. The cool sheets around his body. The hotel room air conditioner humming. The low garble of the TV in the outer room, where Mo was no doubt keeping watch.

His mind, inevitably, went to Jade. He wondered if she slept nude.

Not likely. She rarely relaxed, and she could probably count on the fingers of one hand the number of times she'd been vulnerable to someone else. He pleased himself by deciding he now owned one of those. Would she let them continue? Would she give herself to him again?

Oh, yeah. She would.

He rolled out of bed and headed to the bathroom. After a shower and shave, he dressed and headed out of his room.

Jade and Mo were slouched on the couch and staring at the TV broadcasting the morning news. The smell of coffee permeated the air.

"Breakfast is on the way," she said as he poured himself a shot of much-needed caffeine.

The mug cradled between his hands, he settled into the chair next to the sofa. "Quiet night?"

"Yeah," Mo said. "I've got a report on Garner. I'm waiting for Frank to get up."

"He got back?"

"About three," Mo said.

Seemed as though nobody slept well last night. It was 8:00 a.m., and being a night owl, Remy wasn't exactly crazy about the early hour, but he held a deep appreciation for the sacrifices Jade's team was making so he had no intention of complaining.

"What's for breakfast?" David asked as he strolled out of the other room. In contrast to the rest of them, he looked fresh and rejuvenated.

No one responded, simply pointing at the coffeepot.

Jade shook her head and blew on her coffee as David practically bounced across the room. *Cheerful morning people are a pain in the butt.* He could see the thought cross her mind as if a cartoon word bubble hovered over her.

Either the coffee or her presence managed to wake up his brain. And his libido.

He noted she was wearing her usual jeans and T-shirt—this time in charcoal-gray. Was he imagining the extra flush to her cheeks? Did the glance she gave him hold a special warmth?

Then again, with Jade, it was more likely any warmth or flush could be attributed to anger rather than morning-after joyfulness.

Room service arrived moments later. Jade disengaged the security system, then she and Mo brought two, white-draped, rolling tables into the room themselves. Remy doubted the room service guy was interested in offing him, but he supposed their party of people—not to mention all the electronics equipment—would inspire too much conversation in the hotel kitchen.

Either the smell of food or the noise brought Frank out of his room. Though his eyes were bloodshot, he was dressed in jeans and a crisp white shirt. "'Mornin'."

"Our bird is tucked away?" Jade asked as she scooped scrambled eggs onto her plate.

Since the dining room table was loaded down with equipment, they gathered in the living room and held their plates in their laps.

"Yeah. I've got a rotation of off-duty cops watching him. Easy extra cash for them, since I doubt Hannigan will do anything more than run up his room service tab."

"Mo, what did you find out about Garner? Is he still in San Francisco?"

"Yep. He's been moving between his office and a few galleries. Nothing unusual."

"Does he know we're watching him?" Jade asked.

"I don't think it matters if he does," Remy said. "He's been pretty obvious about his moves. No reason we shouldn't be the same. I'd prefer a face-to-face fight."

Jade's gaze slid to his. Her eyes were full of the determination he valued and depended on. "Me, too."

"He doesn't know," Mo said.

Frank cleared his throat. "I've got some NSA news."

Remy's voice mail had been full of increasingly harsh voice and text messages from his boss, demanding Remy check in. He'd finally complied late last night by sending a text message that he was fine and being well protected. He hadn't turned the phone on this morning and could only imagine the reply he'd received.

"I did some asking around," Frank continued. "A guy I know was recently asked by his supervisor to dig into Remy's business for possible illegal activities."

Remy had always known the agency would betray him. Nobody with any sense would trust a group of spies. Still, the confirmation stung. "Who's the guy?"

Frank shook his head. "Sorry, I shouldn't tell you that."

"The supervisor?" Remy asked, pressing the issue. He deserved to know who was stabbing him in the back.

"Jordan Hillman."

His supervisor. Remy clenched his fist. "A direct order?"

"No, it was passed through another agent, but he later verified it during a phone call."

"What did he find out?"

"He said not much. He told Hillman your art business looked on the up-and-up to him. My buddy didn't like the assignment, though, so he might have held back information."

"I don't see how," Remy said, rising to refill his coffee. He needed to move around, to walk off his anger and resentment. "There's nothing to find."

"Jordan Hillman didn't hire a hit on Remy," Jade said. "Looking at Remy's business is just his usual paranoia. He thinks four steps ahead of everybody and two steps back. He's fishing and hoping for a bite. If he found anything, he wouldn't even tell anybody. He'd just store away the information for a time when he could hold it over Remy's head."

"I'd like to repeat—there's nothing to find." Calmer, Remy returned to his seat and considered that he'd graciously given the NSA four years of his life. Maybe it was time to officially retire from his penance. They'd never be able to prosecute him now. He knew too much about them. "Though Hillman would probably be pissed to see my balance sheets. My profits are definitely on the upswing."

"No doubt," Jade said. "He was furious when I left and had immediate success. He thinks I sold out. Like I defected to the world of capitalism."

"He has no room to judge," Remy said. "He's a silent partner in a major gun supplier that always gets their NSA contract renewed."

Jade turned toward him. "How do you know that?"

Remy just smiled.

"Still, the request itself can't be ignored," Frank said. "Especially since Hillman's in a bad mood these days."

"I won't go to Washington and report like a good solider," Remy said.

"Ignore him," Jade said, her eyes flashing with anger. "We don't need his help, and he just wants to control you."

Remy raised his eyebrows. "Are you suggesting I break the rules?"

"I'm suggesting Hillman's bureaucratic self can cool his heels until we get Garner and figure out how he plays into Remy's past. The ring and its meaning is what we focus on."

"I'm for that," David said.

"So we table the NSA?" Jade asked, her gaze going to Frank.

"As long as we don't let them fall off the radar."

Jade stacked her empty plate with everyone else's, then she and Mo pushed the tables out to the hall.

When she returned, she paced in front of them. "I'm going to call Detective Parker this morning and set up an appointment for Remy to give his statement about last night's attack. Maybe we can get an update on our would-be assaulter, Johnny Malden."

Frank snorted. "Who wound up getting assaulted himself."

"That'll teach him to mess with J.B.," David added.

"David, I want you to connect with the San Francisco police. Let's see what their cops have to say about the slippery Mr. Garner. If they can't find out anything," she added, sensing the question David was bound to ask, "we'll give Detective Parker more. He seems like a good cop, but our client is open to prosecution for past activities. We have to tread carefully."

"Yeah, especially since the bad guy is hiring amateurs," David said.

"Maybe he's a cheapskate," Frank suggested with a smile.

"Maybe," Jade said. "Or maybe he's waiting for us to lower our guard before a big attack. The *real* attack. We're on our toes today, people."

The men nodded and started to rise.

"One more thing before we break," she added, shoving her hands in the back pockets of her jeans.

Her team returned to their seats, and she cast Remy a furtive glance—one full of an odd combination of warmth, regret and embarrassment. Realizing what she was about to do, he stood. "Don't. You don't have to."

"Yes, I do."

10

JADE STILL WASN'T sure how she felt about her relationship with Remy.

It was wrong and right. It was inconvenient and perfectly timed. It was lovely and frustrating. It made her edgy, even as it was satisfying.

But this case wasn't about her feelings. The lives of the men before her depended on her good judgment. She trusted her team, and they gave her the same in return.

Her employees had invariably seen her practically naked— either by proximity or when a disguise was required. They'd put wires down her shirt and taped recorders and monitors to various parts of her body.

There was no place for embarrassment.

She drew a deep breath and launched into the speech she'd rehearsed many times over through the night. "My relationship with our client has gone beyond a professional nature. It's not something I can apologize for, but I ask for your understanding. If any of you feel uncomfortable continuing with this assignment, I need to know now."

The men all exchanged looks, then grinned simultaneously.

"Finally got laid, did you, boss?" David asked.

"I, well, I—" She had. There wasn't much point in denying it.

Frank punched David in the arm—though without much force behind it. "Mind your manners, boy."

Mo frowned at David in disapproval, then surprised her by rising and hugging her briefly. "You need a break from work, and Mr. Tremaine is a good man."

"Oh, well. Thanks."

She felt Remy lay his hand on her shoulder, and she wasn't sure if that helped or made her feel more awkward.

"You treat her right, Mr. Tremaine," Mo said, releasing her as his dark, threatening gaze slid to a point behind her. "I'm gonna get some sleep, boss."

Just like that, it was done. "Sure. Go ahead."

By the time she turned around, Frank and David had re-treated to the computers and were ragging each other about yet another game.

Next to her, Remy slid his hands into his pants pockets. "They're an amazing group."

"Yeah." They were there for her no matter what. Like family. She'd never realized how important that was to her until this moment. "We've got a busy day ahead, so—"

"We're not going to bask in the moment?"

"No."

"Not even for a moment?"

She let her gaze slide over his body. He distracted her like no one else. How she would love to give him her ex-clusive attention.

When the case was over? But then they'd be over, too.

The tender look in his eyes wasn't something she was ready to deal with. She'd been honest, yet she'd taken a step she never thought she would. As was her normal routine, she tempered her feelings with sarcasm. "You're not going to recite poetry, are you?"

"I don't think so."

"Thank God. Let's call the cops."

THROUGHOUT THE DAY, Jade followed up on e-mails and voice messages. She made Frank take a nap. She fed David endlessly. She calmed other skittish clients, who wanted her personal attention for their concerts, movie junkets or book tours. She accompanied her present client to the police station, where they both signed their testimony concerning the attack of the night before.

She waffled from stress to laughter to anger and back again, but recognized the bodyguard profession wasn't exactly revered for its stress-reducing qualities.

She constantly looked to Remy for support and advice, and by the time they'd eaten dinner and returned to work, her head was ready to explode. "Detective Parker is a pain in the butt."

Remy glanced at her over the laptop he was working on. "Maybe we shouldn't get into a deep discussion about law enforcement just now. I'm feeling bitter."

She leaned back into the sofa and stretched her arms over her head. "Your boss launching an internal investigation will do that to you."

"A *private* investigation, don't forget."

"He's just jealous 'cause you're so cute."

Remy grinned. "Cute, huh?" He rose and walked toward her, looking more than cute. More like delicious. "Let's go out for dessert."

"Huh?" Maybe because she'd just thought of him as delicious, she wondered if that was some kind of code word for sex. "Dessert?"

"The sweet part at of the end of the meal."

She shook her head. She was getting punchy. That still sounded suggestive. But he seemed serious about eating. And leaving. "We're not going anywhere."

"We'll just wait for the bad guys to knock on our door?"

"No, but—"

He stood and held out his hand. "Let's go."

So, she found herself tucked into the limo and heading to a place that served dessert. Admittedly, Remy hadn't put a gun to her head, but she was still certain she needed to be a million places besides this one. And when she'd lost control—and her mind—she wasn't really sure, but she definitely had, and when she recovered she'd no doubt be pissed. But for now, she gave herself over to the moment.

"Where are we going? The Cheesecake Factory?"

"No."

"Why not?"

"We're going someplace better."

"My cousin-in-law's bakery, maybe?"

He slid his hand along her thigh. "How'd you guess?"

"This is my security detail, remember? The driver works for me."

Okay, so maybe she hadn't lost *complete* control.

"Plus," she continued, "the only thing other than work that could pull me out of the hotel would be Vanessa's double-chocolate cheesecake." She covered his hand with hers. "And I knew you'd try to get Lucas and me together at some point."

"Am I that transparent?"

"Oh, yeah."

"You shouldn't push him away."

"Because everybody near me is so safe."

"Because he's family."

Her heart contracted. "That was a low blow."

"But it'll be softened by cheesecake."

"Maybe."

She'd already agreed to a huge compromise by letting them leave the hotel alone—except for their driver, Charlie. After last night's attack, she was on edge. But at the same time she relished a fight. As always, she was arrogant enough to think she could beat the bad guys and keep her client safe.

She couldn't imagine why anyone would take on a case without being sure it could be won.

But maybe the lull was part of Garner's plan. He was crafty and quiet, and—if Remy's suspicions were correct—he'd gotten away with murder before. She wasn't sure what had been the trigger and wasn't sure it mattered. Remy had the ring, and Garner would come for it. In person. Eventually.

"I won't be the reason for you and Lucas fighting," Remy said.

"You aren't. I want him to be safe and we aren't safe right now."

"I won't let anything happen to him."

But she knew as well as anybody that things happened to people you loved no matter what you did. Fate crooked its evil finger, and everything changed. Could she have protected her parents the day they'd died?

If she'd run the security plan, would she have changed anything?

Through the NSA, she'd been privy to every detail of the shooting, and she'd eventually determined the protection had been impeccable, the motive unpredictable. The mayor had been an affable guy, loved by his constituents. Eventually, the investigation had determined that his likability had been the motive. The terrorists had thought they would get a lot more attention assassinating a hero than a villain.

Remy must have sensed her mood, because he squeezed her thigh and asked, "So is this cheesecake as good as I've heard?"

"Better."

"I can't wait. Until we get there, though—" he tugged her into his lap "—we could find interesting ways to pass the time."

"We'll be there in five minutes."

He cupped the back of her head. "But I've been waiting all day for this."

His mouth closed over hers, his tongue sweeping inside, firing her senses. Heat shimmered through her body, like a meteor shooting through the sky. She wasn't used to this explosive rise to desire. If she spent a thousand days and nights with him would their passion grow tedious, become routine?

She didn't see how. Everywhere he touched her she burned and longed for more. His body hardened beneath her legs, and she ached for him to fill her, to share skin-on-skin contact, to satisfy the itch he inspired.

She *had* managed to work beside him all day without jumping his body.

But it hadn't been easy.

He squeezed her breast through her shirt. "Maybe we should have skipped dessert."

She cupped him between his legs. "Probably so."

"We're here, Ms. Broussard," Charlie said over the intercom.

Breath heaving, Jade jumped back to her seat as if she'd been shot. He always managed to make her forget where she was, narrowed her world so that only he existed.

"To be continued," he said, kissing the side of her neck as the limo rolled to a stop.

She swallowed and didn't have the nerve to ask if that was a promise or a threat. How did he recover so fast? By the size of the erection she'd been squeezing, he was as needy as she. It was damned embarrassing that she still couldn't catch her breath.

At the back door of the bakery, Jade rolled her shoulders to dispel the lingering edginess and knocked. Vanessa greeted them a moment later, and Jade made introductions between her and Remy.

Although it was conceivable that Vanessa hadn't met all of her husband's business contacts, Jade sensed that the lack of introduction was more likely Remy's decision. No matter how good he was, or how many precautions the NSA took, his life constantly hung in a precarious balance. He didn't share his innermost thoughts. Like her, he kept people at a distance, keeping contact at a minimum and avoiding any involvement with their personal lives. It was an actual job requirement.

Their shared experience was something she'd never imagined she would have with anyone beyond a colleague. It fed their strong, sensual connection. It created a bond.

"You look fine to me," Vanessa said, angling her head of glossy blond hair.

"We are," Jade said as they entered the large, spotless kitchen outfitted with stainless steel appliances, tiled counters lining the room and a huge center island. "Did you think we wouldn't be?"

Vanessa rolled her eyes. "Lucas was full of life-threatening drama."

"We have had plenty of life-threatening drama, but that's not exactly abnormal in my business."

"Well, have some cheesecake." She extended her arm toward the island, where two plates containing thick slices were resting. "Lucas will be along any moment."

They dug into the dessert, while Vanessa kneaded a huge roll of cinnamon-scented dough.

"You're not having any?" Jade asked, picking up her fork.

"Ugh. I've made sweets for three bachelorette parties, four retirement parties and five kiddie birthdays this week. I'm sick to death of chocolate."

Jade shoveled the first luscious bite in her mouth and nearly moaned. "That's even better than I remember," she said when she'd swallowed. Her normal day involved guns and surveillance systems. Vanessa's consisted of sugar, chocolate and more sugar and chocolate.

It was a weird, weird world.

"Thanks." Vanessa's gaze went to Remy. "Are you…okay?"

"I need a minute to myself to fully appreciate the complexity of this dish."

Jade glanced at him to see that his eyes were closed. His face was flushed. His expression bordered on orgasmic. Clearly, the allure of chocolate wasn't limited to women.

Pleased that she'd finally found a weak spot in him, Jade went back to devouring her own slice of cheesecake.

"So, Remy, you're an art dealer, right?" Vanessa asked.

"I am. Mostly I commission work for my clients. Say somebody wants a certain type of painting or sculpture, or a specific work from an artist. I find it, and either buy it myself, or negotiate a deal between owner and potential buyer."

"Let me guess—you're responsible for that weird naked man bronze sculpture in our apartment?"

"The Christopher Hagan? Yes."

Vanessa shook her head in amazement. "The things you boys can find to waste money on."

"He's the premier bronze sculptor of the twentieth century."

"Well, he should have taken anatomy class before he went to art school. Legs don't grow out of ears."

Jade bit back a grin at the startled look of offense on Remy's face.

"At least bronzes are a better investment than the traditional boys' toys like boats or sports cars," he said.

"Or planes," Jade said dryly.

He hunched over his cheesecake and said nothing.

"So what happened?" Vanessa asked. "Why'd somebody shoot you? You sell a guy a fake van Gogh, or something?"

Jade and Remy exchanged a cautious look. They couldn't discuss the specifics of the case with anybody outside their security team. Though when Lucas arrived—as Remy's attorney—they could go into detail about some things. Lucas would certainly demand all the information he could get, and he was a highly intelligent man. It couldn't hurt to have another opinion on Peter Garner.

As long as they left out any mention of the NSA, she didn't see any harm in sharing anything in Remy's past he felt comfortable talking about.

"No, it has something to do with Remy's past," she said. "We'll tell you all about it when Lucas gets here."

The subject of violence and mayhem aside, they talked about food. Vanessa was working on new recipes for a Turtle cheesecake, a key lime and raspberry tart and a peanut butter pie. Jade's stomach rumbled the entire time, and Remy looked at Vanessa as if she were some amazing goddess who had floated out of the sky.

She also shared her recent successes with bridal teas and luncheons. She told them Christmas was always one of her busiest times of the year, but this past year it was not just busy, but wild. One executive of a computer graphics firm had imbibed too much from the open bar and wound up doing a naked Elvis impersonation on a conference table.

It was so refreshing to hear somebody talk about everyday events. *Normal* life. Jade had long ago come to terms with the fact that her life would never be that way, so it was wonderful to have moments like these. She was glad Lucas was happy and had found such a wonderful woman to share his life with.

When her cousin finally arrived, he kissed and embraced his wife, shook Remy's hand then glared at her.

She crossed her arms over her chest and glared back. The man really needed to get over this little tantrum.

"Oh, good grief," Vanessa said. She grabbed Lucas's hand, then Jade's, then forced them to hold hands. "Both of you are too stubborn for your own good."

"I can't talk about some parts of my business with you," she said.

His green eyes hardened even further. "I thought you trusted me."

"It's not a matter of trust. My clients expect and get their privacy. And, in some cases, too much knowledge can be dangerous. I already don't like the connection between you and Remy."

"I don't advertise my client list, for God's sake."

"Somebody could have seen you together. They know you know each other."

"*They* who?"

She shook her head and released his hand, stepping back

from him and his anger. The NSA kept very close tabs on their agents. They had to know Remy and Lucas did business together. And while NSA agents were the best snoopers she knew, if they could find out, somebody else might be able to, as well. She'd worked in the underground world of spies too long not to know paranoia saved lives.

"There are some things you can't know," she said.

"Then what are you doing here?" Lucas asked, his voice hard.

"It was *his* idea," she said, pointing at Remy. "We'd like your *opinion*. We're not calling you in for duty."

"We think the shooting may be related to an incident from my past," Remy said. "My childhood."

Lucas's gaze slid to Remy, then back to Jade. His expression softened. She knew there were ghosts floating around his past. "Trips down memory lane aren't always easy."

Remy shrugged. "No, they're not."

Lucas walked over to the cabinet. He pulled down a bottle of whiskey and two glasses, then poured a small amount in each glass. "I know you won't have any, Jade," he said as he handed Remy one of the glasses. "Vanessa, you want some wine?"

"Sure, why not?"

After Remy dragged over a couple more stools and Lucas delivered the drinks—he poured Jade a diet soda that she thought might be their first step toward reconciliation—her client grinned. "You see, I wasn't always an art dealer...."

By the time he finished his story, Vanessa's jaw had dropped, and Lucas's eyes were glinting with a weird sort of pride. He'd boosted a car or two in his day. It was probably some sort of criminal-brothers-in-arms bonding thing to know that your client also used to steal stuff.

"Well, I'll be damned," Vanessa said.

"No, I probably will," Remy said, "though the good sisters continue to encourage me to repent."

"So why would Garner point so obviously to himself?" Vanessa asked, the same question Jade had asked herself many times over. "Why did he call you? Why would he identify himself to that guy who tried to attack you outside the club? He could have given him any name. Or no name."

"Honestly," Jade said, gathering everyone's plates and glasses and heading to the dishwasher, "we don't have a clue."

"He *wants* me to know it's him," Remy said.

Vanessa shook her head. "But why—"

"To rattle you," Lucas said.

Jade turned toward him. Lucas used to be an A-plus rattler, so he'd know how it was done. And it made a weird kind of sense.

"An attempt on your life would raise your public profile," she said. "Smoke you out into the open."

"Knock you off balance and distract you," Lucas added.

"And it would bring me to the attention of the police— whom he knows I'd rather keep a low profile with."

"He wants that ring," Jade said. "He's pissed you wouldn't sell it to him, so now he's hoping you'll be shaken up enough by the attacks that you'll be willing to give it up."

"I agree," Lucas said, sliding his hands into his pockets and staring at her. "Sometime in the next week, he'll contact you and offer the money again. Or maybe a trade."

She knew Lucas would offer a fresh perspective, even if she was a little leery of letting him get too involved. "Remy's life for the ring."

Her cousin was friends with Remy, so he undoubtedly didn't like the sound of that. Jade wondered if anybody realized how scary that idea was to her. She didn't see how, since she hadn't realized it herself until this moment, as her stomach bottomed out and her hands trembled.

She fisted them and shook away the image of Remy lying on a cold slab in the morgue. She wouldn't let down her client or her team. Remy's life would be back to normal, and she'd go back to work. That was the way she and Remy had agreed things would be.

That's what she still wanted, wasn't it?

Yes. No matter how physically compatible she and Remy were, they were complete opposites in many other ways. The fact that he'd been a thief went against every sense of order and rightness she'd ever known.

"Oh, boy," Remy said with a dramatic eye roll. "Now all I have to do is cool my heels, twiddle my thumbs and wait around for a killer to pop out from behind a bush and invite me to play *Let's Make a Deal*."

A clattering sound reverberated from beyond the back door.

Jade drew her pistol and stalked over. "You expecting anybody?" she asked Vanessa quietly.

"No." Her voice sounded more confused than fearful. "My partner's out of town with her boyfriend."

"Everybody duck down behind the island," she said. "Everybody," she added when Remy drew his revolver from his ankle holster.

He positioned himself on the other side of the door, and she sighed. He was trained, after all. She just wasn't used to her clients jumping in to assist in their own protection.

The doorknob shook, and the low rumble of voices echoed.

She knew without looking over that her cousin hadn't ducked. He was staying put, though, and she was grateful for that at least. She moved her gaze to Remy's. He nodded his readiness, then he focused on the door.

Why had she exposed Lucas and Vanessa to danger? Had the NSA decided to take Remy back forcibly? Had Garner followed them? And why hadn't Charlie warned them?

She took a deep breath and waited.

When the door flew open, Jade stepped in front of the intruder and pointed her weapon with deadly intent.

The shocked, dark-haired woman collapsed in a dead faint into the arms of the equally shocked man behind her. This was no attack. These people were not paid muggers, assassins or government agents.

"Ah, Jade," Vanessa said from behind her, "that's my partner. Oh, and her boyfriend."

11

"YOU PEOPLE ARE seriously disturbed."

Remy chuckled at the furious glare in the eyes of Vanessa's feisty and exotic partner, Mia.

She smiled at Remy. "Though *you* are seriously cute."

The woman's live-in boyfriend, Colin, was sitting beside her, patting her hand at the time this comment was made.

The normalcy of the whole situation was refreshing, and he was sure Jade felt the same. Vanessa plied her partner with wine. Lucas produced a barstool that he assisted Mia onto.

As Mia ranted about guns and unprovoked violence and the general lousy state of the world, even stalwart Jade—who'd pulled the gun that started the whole business in the first place—cracked a smile. By the time they escaped, Jade and Lucas had shared a healing smile and Remy had made off with several more pieces of the luscious cheesecake.

"I'm hiding it," he said as they pulled out of the parking lot, holding the precious plastic container next to his chest. "And if you tell anybody else, I'm firing you."

Jade glanced at him out of the corner of her eye. "It's chocolate and cream cheese."

"Oh, no. It's way more than that."

"Okay back there?" Charlie asked.

The poor man had been humiliated when he'd learned what

had happened after Mia's unexpected entrance. Vanessa's partner had confronted him in the limo when she'd pulled in, asking him what he was doing lurking in the alley. Charlie had said he was only waiting for a client and had given Jade's name, which Mia recognized. Mia assured him she was a part owner of the property. She had a key, so he hadn't considered warning them of her approach.

"We're fine, Charlie," Jade said as she pressed the speaker button. "Let it go. If every false alarm is that entertaining, I'm all for it." She turned to Remy. "You, however, have serious issues. The last time we were alone in this limo *I* was in your lap, not that cake."

Remy glanced down at the precious container. "Yeah, so?"

"I'm getting passed over for chocolate?"

"You can share me." He grinned. "In fact, I could spread this amazing dessert all over your body." He leaned close, absorbing her softness and alluring scent. "Then I could lick it off."

She trailed her fingers through his hair, and his body reacted by constricting, then throbbing. "*Now* you're talking."

But before they could make further plans, her cell phone rang. When she hit the speaker button, Frank's voice floated out.

"New development with Garner. He's going to be attending an art showing here in Atlanta in three days. Coincidence?"

Remy's gaze locked with Jade's.

"No way."

BY THE TIME they returned to the suite, Mo was awake and David hadn't yet gone to bed, so everyone was present for the strategy meeting.

Remy's senses were fired. He could practically picture the

coming showdown. Though he was thinking more like *The Thomas Crowne Affair* than a shootout at the O.K. Corral.

"Maybe we should go to San Francisco tonight and catch *him* off guard for once," David said.

Remy liked that plan. He wanted to face Garner, end this surprise attack crap and find out what was so damn important about that ring. Garner didn't really want to kill him. He wasn't hiring a local yahoo like Johnny Malden for a hit.

Lucas was right—Garner was trying to throw him off balance.

"No," Jade said, pacing as usual. "That's his territory."

"We're gonna invite him to The Big Easy?" Frank asked in disbelief.

"We're good here," she said. "Remy knows Atlanta, he knows the art world and the underground criminal and law enforcement element. We only have three days. We need that time to plan. Do you know this gallery where the opening is being held?" she asked Remy.

"Very well."

"Can you get us the blueprints? Can we get some of our people in place of the security guards or caterer's staff?"

"I do business with the owner often but I wouldn't necessarily trust him, especially since Garner obviously knows about the gallery." He picked up the brochure advertising the showing and ran down the list of artists. "He's coming an awfully long way for a viewing of medium-quality work."

"He's practically waving a red flag with this appearance here," David said. "He'll be expecting us. Why go undercover?"

"But I don't think he realizes we already know he's coming," Frank said. "My information came through a private source." He and Jade exchanged a telling look.

As he had been from the first, Remy was impressed with

their discretion and professionalism. To be successful in their business, you had to have contacts in law enforcement, PIs, other security companies. Add in their NSA connections—especially Frank's, who'd put twenty years into the agency—and they'd undoubtedly developed a vast network of informants.

If Frank thought they were one step ahead of Garner, Remy believed him. "He wants me at that opening, though, so he'll announce officially that he's coming the day before— probably with an article in the newspaper."

"How do you know that?" Mo asked.

"It's what I would do," Remy said.

"He's as smart as you?" David asked, sounding concerned.

"I wouldn't go that far," he said with a modest smile. "And I don't *know* what he'll do, I just suspect."

"If he wants this ring so badly, why hasn't he tried to steal it?" David asked.

"Oh, please," Jade said.

Mo shook his head.

"Oh, right," David said. "Sorry, Mr.—ah, Remy. Of course, with your skills, he couldn't—"

"*Don't* compliment his skills," Jade said with a pointed glare. When her gaze slid to Remy's, her eyes held a hint of heat. "Such as they are."

Remy swallowed his smile. "The thing to remember is that the ring is just a means to an end. A key to something more important."

"To what?" Clearly frustrated they couldn't find the answer to that all-important question, Jade shoved her hands in the back pockets of her jeans. "And how does Garner know when you don't?"

"Maybe he just found out," Frank said.

"But from whom?" Mo said. "Everybody else is dead."

"When we meet, this will all come to an end." Remy was certain he could feel the ring burning in his pocket. "I think I can even reason with him, get him to split the profits of whatever is on the other end."

Jade's gaze jumped to his. "So we just forget all about the *you tried to kill me* business?

"I didn't say that." In fact—after he got the information he needed—he wouldn't rest until Garner was in jail or dead. He'd gotten away with his crimes for too long. Maybe Remy's father had been a thief, but he hadn't deserved to die. Garner, one way or another, had caused his death, and it was long past time he paid for it.

"You don't really think you can talk to him rationally," she said.

"Probably not." He rose to pour himself more coffee. "But it could be fun trying."

She huffed out a disgusted breath. "Fun."

He glanced back at her. "And you're not invited. You'll get pissed, shoot him, then we'll never know where all this leads."

"Oh, but I will be there. And if Garner goes down, then he does. You'd be out of danger. That's my job."

The finality of her words struck him oddly. She'd be gone soon. He'd be alone again. Even though that was their agreement, he didn't want to keep it. Had he ever intended to?

He walked toward her. "Your job—to close the case and move on."

"Yes."

The air in the room thickened with tension that had nothing to do with the case. He and Jade had made this personal for themselves and everyone else. They'd done it with their eyes wide open, but had either of them been prepared for the results?

He certainly hadn't expected to want to protect her, to actually feel a stab of fear as he'd watched her draw her weapon earlier tonight. To wonder if they'd be quick enough, clever enough to beat Garner and survive.

"So Garner is going to offer his bribe again. What are you going to tell him?" Frank asked, breaking the awkward silence.

"Let's make a deal," Remy said.

"And if he makes trouble, we'll be ready," Mo said, his dark eyes narrowed.

Personally, if Remy were the bad guy, he'd run the other direction from the massive Mo. But some people seemed destined for trouble. Peter Garner was going to run into a handful with this team.

"He might use force instead of cash," Mo continued.

"Leverage," David added.

"Somebody close to you," Frank said, leaning forward.

Remy refused to look at Jade. "I don't have anybody close to me."

"*Lucas,*" Jade said quietly, her face paling for a moment.

Remy shook his head. "Don't even think it. No one knows about our relationship." He thought about the NSA. Well, maybe somebody did. But not Garner.

His life was circling around, chasing him, demanding he set what was wrong right again. At almost all costs, but not at the expense of friends.

He rose and approached her, cupping her elbows in his hands. "I wouldn't risk Lucas. I wouldn't."

But he had. Just by picking him, by letting him into his life, he had. At the time he'd arranged the meeting, his curiosity about Jade had been eating him from the inside out. Later, he'd decided he was being clever by retaining an attorney who was connected to somebody who knew the inner workings of the NSA. Eventually, he'd gained a respect and appreciation for Lucas on his own.

She lifted her head and met his gaze. "I know."

Relief rolled through him. Her opinion of him was fast becoming a thorny aspect of their relationship. He couldn't wave away or dismiss the idea that they stood on opposite sides of the fence in many respects. They were supposed to be about curiosity and chemistry, about release and satisfying physical needs.

They had become much more.

"We ought to give Garner somebody to take," Frank said, leaning back in his chair.

"Oh, *really?*" Jade asked, jamming her hands on her hips. "Who?"

"Me."

"No. No way." She tossed her hands in the air. "Are you people determined to make me crazy today?"

Frank stood, jutting his chin forward. "What if he knows about Lucas, Jade? I won't let you lose the only family you have left. I can handle myself with Garner."

Her body was equally stiff with anger. "Unless he shoots you in the head the moment he has you."

"Sacrificing one of us isn't the way," Mo said.

"I agree," Remy said. Frank was just as much family to Jade as Lucas was. Though no one member of the team was more precious than the other. If anybody should be taken, it was him. And he wasn't feeling that sacrificial.

Jade nodded. "*Finally,* the voices of reason."

"I'll go," Remy said jokingly, since that would accomplish nothing. Garner would have all the cards.

Jade cut her gaze toward him. "Think again."

"I'll go to the *showing*. With all of you hovering two inches from me." He smiled. "Let's stick together, shall we? I think we make a pretty good team."

Frank hunched his shoulders. "Fine." He dropped into his chair.

"Let's move back to the plan," Mo said.

"Here, here," Remy said, setting aside his coffee cup. "We may not be able to get on with the staff at the gallery, but we do have a connection we can trust. Vanessa."

Jade shook her head. "No. Lucas is bad enough, but—"

"I don't mean use her personally. The gallery is bound to have a catering service contracted. We can find out who that is, and Vanessa can help us by calling that company and asking if her cousin *David*—who's an expert waiter—can earn some extra money for the night.

"Security-wise Mo is the man. He's big, he's obvious, he's scary."

Mo smiled, though he didn't look much less intimidating. "Hey, but I like puppies and bunny rabbits."

"Let's just keep that to ourselves for the time being," Remy said carefully, wondering if he liked to eat them or pet them.

"So, I have Mo at my side. Some of my art colleagues will no doubt be surprised by the security measures, but I can tell them all my amazing story of nearly being shot, and that will create an interesting buzz and distraction for the party."

"This is good," Jade said, staring down at him with a new kind of respect in her eyes.

Remy basked in her praise but tried not to be obvious. "If

it works." He gestured toward Frank, who was still sulking. "Frank can either be a party guest or he can do surveillance in a van outside."

"What am I?" Jade asked, standing in front of him and scowling. "Your empty-headed date again?"

"Date, yes." He grabbed her hand and pulled her into his lap. "Empty-headed, definitely not."

Frank, grinning at them, stood and clapped his hands. "Okay, boys, time for us to get busy." He winked at Remy. "Somewhere else."

Jade wriggled out of Remy's lap. "No, *boys,* we have lots to—"

"What?" Frank spread his hands. "We've got a few phone calls to make. I've got a tux to rent. I'll be good as a wealthy art patron. Just like the old days." He paused and angled his head. "But there is some new surveillance equipment I've been planning to test. Hmm, well, whichever role I choose it's a good plan."

Jade glared at him. "Until Lucas gets wind of what we're up to, and he and Vanessa show up."

Frank waved off her concerns. "We'll protect them, J.B. They'll add some authenticity. Members of the local community and all."

"No. I don't like it."

"Come on, we—"

"You've been hanging around him too long," she said, jerking her head toward Remy. "We're not weaving outside the lines. We're doing this on our own."

"You're being overly protective," Frank said.

"I'm not. I'm just following a straight path."

"Which isn't always the best."

Watching their standoff, Remy felt guilt creep over him. He didn't want to be responsible for a conflict between partners. "Can we table this 'til tomorrow?" he asked, standing and stretching. "We have the basics, and I could use some sleep before I figure out the rest."

Grumbling and shuffling ensued, but after David and Frank agreed on a movie to watch in the other room, and Mo had his generous bowl of cookie-dough ice cream to entertain him as he watched a reality show in the main room, Remy managed to snag Jade's hand and discreetly slip into his room.

He leaned back against the door and watched her pace. Her mind was obviously busy with the plan he had proposed. She was looking for holes and weaknesses, which she'd undoubtedly do until the moment they arrived at the gallery.

He, however, wasn't thinking about work. He was thinking about getting her away. Of finding out what was really between them, how far they could explore each other, and he'd never get another opportunity after the case was resolved.

This was his moment, and he intended to take it.

You have a plane, man. Gas it up and go....

She could plan and pace anywhere, and he could come up with continually inventive ways to distract her. Maybe his fatalistic attitude was flippant and wrong, but he'd lived on the edge too long to not appreciate the sunrise and sunset, to take passion where he could find it and to always long for more. He needed Jade's touch. He longed for her respect.

Maybe he'd get one or both.

"Am I really such a horrible influence?" he asked her as she paced in front of him for what had to be the tenth time.

She stopped and planted her hands on her hips. "What are you talking about?"

"You know what I mean. *You've been hanging around him too long.*"

"You're aware we have different approaches."

"But as long as we get the job done, does it really matter how we get there?"

"Hell, yes."

They'd likely never be *in simpatico* there. But maybe they could still be together. Maybe they could find a way to compromise and have some semblance of peace when their professional lives had them stressed to the hilt. Could they turn to each other then? Could they share more than just passion?

He walked toward her, pulling her into his arms. "Can we forget the case for now?"

"Can't do that," she said, though she laid her head against his chest and sighed.

"How about we set it aside, then? Just for a little while. You can pick apart my plan all you want later." He stroked his hand down her arm. "Right now, I'd rather touch you. I'd prefer you smile at me instead of scowl." He leaned back a bit so he could see her face. She obligingly smiled, though not too broadly. He dipped his head, stopping a breath away from her lips. "I'd rather kiss you," he whispered.

Which he did, by nibbling gently at her lower lip. Then he slid his tongue slowly, oh, so slowly, around her top lip. When he covered her mouth completely with his and she trembled, he knew he had her.

Jade curled her fingertips into Remy's shirt and closed her eyes as his lips moved over hers.

Whenever he touched her, she forgot her sense of time and place. She could only focus on him, on the way he made her feel and the way she wanted to make him feel in return. As much as she didn't want to admit it, she was relieved when he forced her to let go of her job. She couldn't seem to do so on her own.

It was equally—maybe doubly—as nice that she had him, in particular, to turn to for a distraction.

His heart pounded against her wrist as her own pulse picked up speed like a racehorse stretching to the finish line. He molded her hips against his, and his erection made her body grow damp and needy.

The stroke of his tongue against hers sent her senses soaring, her head swimming. No other man had ever made her want so much, to long to spend hours—maybe even days— exploring his body while he explored hers. Kissing had never seemed so important. Touching had never been vital. Sex had never been a priority.

But at the same time, he scared her. What if she couldn't stop thinking about him when she was supposed to be working? What if her body grew so used to him that she craved him all the time?

Dependence seemed the ultimate handicap. Relying on a man who wouldn't be around for more than a week seemed foolish.

"Remy, what are we doing?" she asked as he lifted his head.

"About to climb into that bed and get naked?"

She looked into his eyes—silvery and charged and wonderfully full of expectation—and wanted nothing more in the world than to do just that. "Sounds perfect."

Turning them around, she shoved him lightly onto the mattress, then began unbuttoning his shirt. "I really like your chest," she said as she pushed his shirt down his shoulders.

"You do?" His eyebrows lifted. "Feel free to explore all you like."

She knelt between his legs and kissed him, just over his heart. It beat strong and sure beneath her lips, and she fought against the idea that somebody wanted to stop its life-giving force. The ring might be the mission, but getting rid of Remy was the ultimate goal.

She wouldn't let it happen. She hadn't been able to save her parents, but she'd saved many, many people since. She hadn't lost a client yet, and Remy definitely wouldn't be the first.

When she tongued his nipple, he sucked in a quick breath and laid his hand on the back of her head. Her own nipples contracted, hardening to aching peaks and pushing against her cotton bra.

She kissed and licked her way slowly down the center of his chest, just along his sternum, between his tightened abdominal muscles. When she reached the waistband of his pants, she paused and looked up at him. She kept her gaze locked with his as she felt along his belt loop and unhooked it. She unbuttoned his pants, unzipped the fly, then slid her hand into his underwear and grasped his erection in her hand.

His eyes slid closed. His stomach contracted. His breathing grew labored.

She turned her attention to his penis and stroked up, then down, and he hardened further, pulsing against her palm. She knew from experience with her own body that the friction of a firm hand, balanced with a gentle touch, heightened every sensation and stimulated desire like touching a live electrical wire.

The head of his penis stood out, flushed red with blood rushing beneath the surface. A spot of fluid hovered on top, nd she dipped her finger in it and tapped her tongue. The salty aste was *essence de Remy*. She nearly giggled at the thought.

"Don't stop now," he said, his voice strained.

"Mmm." She gazed at his burgeoning cock. "I have no intention of doing that."

As she slid her mouth over the top, she relaxed her throat, o she could take him deeper.

The number of times she'd done this were *extremely* few nd far between, but criminals liked to watch porn, so she'd een her fair share of the experts at work during night surveilance. She mimicked the actors' pose, bracing her hands gainst the bed, arching her back and moving up and down vith varying speeds.

As she slowed, she dipped her tongue in the crease. Each ime, he lifted his hips, pressing himself deeper, urging her to ake more. Her palms dampened at the thought of the pleasure he was giving him. Her own desire heightened.

Suddenly, he grasped her beneath her arms and pulled her p, kissing her hard, crushing her body against him. "Off," he aid, panting. "Clothes off."

If she hadn't been so needy herself she might have laughed t the way the usually articulate Remy was at a loss for clever vords. Instead, she lurched to her feet and started tearing off very article of clothing she could reach.

When they were both naked, their gazes connected for a rief second, then he tugged her toward him, and they toppled nto the bed. Lips and teeth scraped across skin as he reached or the nightstand drawer and the condoms. And though she eally wanted to take her time and tease him slowly, rolling he protection over him herself, she let him make the quick, amiliar moves because she sensed his urgency, and she was pretty sure she was going to lose her mind if she didn't have him inside her in the next three seconds.

She lifted her hips and plunged down on him, her breath rushing from her body and her body moaning in relief. "Oh, that's better," she said, breathless, but wriggling her hips to position her thighs comfortably on either side of him and getting just the angle of penetration she wanted.

Rolling back her shoulders, she sat upright.

His hands gripped her waist. His face was a mask of pleasured torture as he gazed up at her. "Do I have any chance of you moving quickly?"

She shifted her hips from side to side. He winced. She smiled and braced her palms against his sweaty chest. "Nope. I like it up here." But she mercifully lifted her hips, then sank down again. "I may stay a while."

"You're killing me."

She angled her head. "I think I've heard that somewhere before."

"Gun range." He bumped his hips against hers, driving himself deeper inside. "You wanted to shoot things, I wanted you just like this."

"Then you should be happy."

"Oh, I—"

She rocked her hips forward and back. "I can't let you suffer." She leaned down, sliding her tongue up the side of his neck, lightly sinking her teeth into his earlobe. "I want to please you."

He groaned. "You are."

She pumped her hips against his. "Tease you."

"You're doing that, too."

She slid her hands down his sweat-soaked sides. A craving

need for completion, for an end to the tension chased her. She planted her hands on the mattress. "Then there's only one thing left to do." Smiling, she rolled her hips and straightened. "Finish you."

Then, she moved quickly.

She thrust her hips, not in an effort to tease and prolong, but to satisfy. The itch crawling up her spine spread, and Remy sighed. They needed to reach that peak, they *had* to go over. Relief was on the other side. The tension and tightening would end. Pleasure would burst. Hearts would sigh.

She arched her neck and back, feeling the roar of satisfaction pushing her. Drawing a deep breath, she absorbed the scent of him, the spicy, sophisticated cologne he wore, as well as the aroma of them together. Simple, elusive, needy.

Closing her eyes, she gave herself to him, her body stretching, her hunger pulsing. She jerked her hips one last time and exploded, the ripples of satisfaction shimmering and trembling through her body, even as he still pushed to completion. She marveled at his control and accepted gladly the bumps and groans as he reached his own peak.

He was an amazing man.

He was a challenge.

He was beautiful.

She flopped on his chest, trying to catch her breath, smiling as the ripples of her orgasm pulsed through her.

They were together for such a short time, she realized with a touch of sadness. As quickly as they could find satisfaction in each other's body, she wanted to slow down and enjoy the ride, to enjoy every moment, draw out every slow kiss.

She sighed, relishing his heart beating, the thumps growing

slower by the moment, lulling her to sleep. Relying on him probably wasn't wise. But, for now, she didn't care. Her eyes fluttered closed, and she let go.

For once.

12

JADE AWOKE NAKED, her back pressed to Remy's bare front.

She had to leave. There was no telling what time it was, and her conscience was screaming about work that needed to be done and plans to be made.

But her body was tired even as her mind raced.

She recalled him asking, last night, if it really mattered how they closed the case, as long as they closed it. The old end-justifies-the-means mind-set. She hated it. Jordan Hillman and nearly all upper levels of the NSA played that game daily.

And when Senator Kilpatrick—whom she'd believed had been the first honest politician she'd ever met—had revealed his illegal activities and made his plea deal, she'd finally had enough.

Remy had taken a deal to save himself, but she understood that. Was that a double standard? Why did she dislike Hillman so much and like Remy?

As for his thievery, she knew she *should* judge him. He'd taken what wasn't his, and there wasn't too much more wrong than that. Yet she respected the man he'd become. Maybe she hadn't at first, but she'd grown to know more than just his body over the last few days.

He was honorable and loyal to his friends. He'd protected

his date the night of the shooting, then done the same for his informant buddy. He remained devoted to the nuns who'd raised him.

Despite his former profession, he was honest. He'd shared his past with her—the good and the bad. He'd been up front about his attraction to her. He'd laid out the agreement of a temporary affair and hadn't played games or pretended they were going to ride off into the sunset together.

She liked his sense of humor, and the way he treated her team. She appreciated his strength and the reverence he held for beautiful things.

But they came to an impasse regarding right and wrong, black and white.

Did that really matter? Their relationship was temporary, fleeting, even. Did he have to agree with her view of the world, or she with his?

Well, she certainly wasn't going to answer that question or solve this case lying in bed. When she started to roll away, Remy pulled her back.

"Don't go," he said groggily.

"It's late."

"It's early—way too early."

"How early?"

He covered her eyes with his other hand. "Don't look."

She sighed. "How will I know what time it is?"

He slid his hand between her legs. "It's time for this."

Instantly wet, she sucked in a breath. Her muscles clenched around his finger. His featherlight touch teased and had her teetering on the edge of satisfaction in seconds. She panted when he inserted one finger just inside her.

"Let's get away for a few days."

It took her several moments to figure out what he'd said. "Be serious."

"I am."

"We have—" she choked when he pressed his finger directly on her clitoris "—plans to…make."

"We can make them in Bermuda," he said, moving her hair off her neck, his breath teasing her skin.

"No, I—"

He pinched her between his fingers, rolling the ultrasensitive skin until she was gasping for air. "When the case is over, we're over, right?"

"I, ah…yes."

"It's almost over. I want some time with you before then."

Her heart kicked in her chest. It *was* almost over. Hadn't she just been thinking the same thing? Why did hearing him say that bother her? "Remy, we can't—"

"I want you to myself." He moved his finger in a slow circle. "We need this."

I need you to move your finger faster! she wanted to scream.

"I'll think about it," she finally said, desperate and on edge.

He kissed the side of her neck and mercifully rubbed his finger back and forth. "Just think how often you could feel this way."

She closed her eyes and angled her hips to give him better access. "Uh, huh."

Finally, *finally,* he must have decided he'd tortured her long enough. He massaged faster and harder. He slicked his fingers in her moisture and applied just enough pressure to get her breath hitching.

Trembling, her muscles tightened. Then she exploded, her body pulsing, grasping for that last stab of pleasure.

Before she'd drawn a decent breath of relief, he'd rolled on a condom and flipped her to her back. He drove himself deep inside her, and her desire shot up again. Her hips lifted, bumping against his as her back and neck arched.

He was going to kill her.

Funny, she always thought she'd take a bullet, not die of hunger, need, passion and pleasure.

Above her, he was hot and strong. She could smell his seductively spicy scent, mixed with sex and need. It was stimulating and mind-fuzzing at the same time.

He wasted no time pushing them to the peak. He moved his hips quickly, angling her body for the deepest penetration. She exploded again, pulsing around him, and he moaned, obviously feeling her orgasm.

He came moments later, pumping his hips a few final times, then collapsing on top of her, his heart hammering against her sweat-soaked chest.

When he'd recovered his breath, he laid on his side next to her and stroked his finger down her nose. "Let's go to the beach."

Shaking her head, Jade rolled off the bed. Instead of being sated like her body, her mind was jumping. She needed to get a close look at the gallery blueprints ASAP. Mo's report was also a priority. He liked to surf the Internet late at night to keep his mind alert, and he always came up with interesting information no one else found.

She scanned the floor for her clothes and found them crumpled at the end of the bed. She tossed them on, knowing she needed to get a shower and dress in fresh clothes before meeting with her team.

Turning, she noted Remy had crawled back under the sheets. "What are you doing?"

"Going back to sleep."

She glanced at the bedside clock. "It's seven-thirty."

He closed his eyes. "Exactly."

She tucked in her shirt and hoped she looked reasonably decent. There was no way she could get to her room without Mo seeing her.

Her hand was wrapped around the doorknob when he spoke from behind her.

"You might want to pack light for our trip."

She glanced over her shoulder at him. "What trip?"

"To the beach."

"I'm not."

"You said you would."

"I said I'd think about it."

He opened his eyes and propped himself on his elbows. "And have you?"

"No."

"Then you forfeit, and I win. Start packing."

"No."

"If I pick your wardrobe, there won't be one. You might want to be more prepared."

She ignored him and strode from the room. *The beach*. The man had lost his mind. She wasn't strolling off to the beach to let her team finish up those pesky little details like planning the encounter with Garner, solving the mystery of the ring and trapping the bad guy.

"'Morning," she said to Mo as she headed to the coffeepot.

"Got some updates for you," he said, not looking up from his laptop screen.

"Let me shower, then we'll get to them."

By the time she'd changed, Frank was up. The two of them sat across from Mo at the dining room table to hear his news.

"This Garner guy has a thing for van Gogh," he said.

"A thing?"

"He has a yacht called *Starry, Starry Night*. His estate is called *Sunflowers*. He owns a couple of van Gogh works, he's a regular at The Met in New York and the van Gogh museum in Amsterdam. Plus he has an entire room in his house devoted exclusively to reproductions of his most famous paintings."

"That's a thing, all right," Jade said.

She heard the door behind her open and turned to see Remy, freshly showered and dressed impeccably, his black hair still damp and curling at his temples. He'd been sleepy-eyed, groggy and naked the last time she'd seen him. He was so damn gorgeous, she couldn't decide which way she preferred him.

"Garner has a thing for van Gogh?" she asked him as he walked toward the coffee station.

"His estate is named after one of his paintings," he said, pouring coffee into a mug, "and he's rumored to have a couple of his drawings, though I've never seen them personally. But he also favors Renoir and Degas."

Mo repeated the information he'd learned.

Remy pulled out a chair and sat next to Jade. His cologne wafted toward her, scattering her thoughts. "Interesting."

"Then there are two weird coincidences," Mo said. "One, many years ago Garner donated a collection of paintings and sculptures to The High Museum of Art here in Atlanta. Two, the museum is getting two of van Gogh's European paintings—" he glanced down at his notes "—*Irises* and *Oleanders* for a month-long loan from The Met in New York." His gaze slid to hers. "The exhibit opens the day after the gallery showing."

"Many years ago he donated works to the museum here? How many years, exactly?"

Mo smiled. "Twenty. Exactly one month after Sean Nagel's death."

Jade glanced at Remy. Clearly, he hadn't known this. "We need a list of the items taken during the job Nagel pulled all those years ago."

"You think Garner donated stolen goods to the museum?" Frank asked.

"Why not?" she said. "The guy doesn't seem to lack balls."

"They could be overpaints," Remy said.

"What's an overpaint?" she asked.

"Sometimes when a piece of art is stolen, the thief will have someone paint over the original so that he can display the piece in the open without revealing the real painting."

"Why in the world would you steal a piece of art you couldn't look at?"

"It's like a private joke. A secret the thief can laugh about only with himself."

She could definitely see some of the people she'd tracked down through the NSA giggling themselves silly over hidden, stolen art. "And the sculptures?"

"You put them inside a bigger sculpture."

"We need that list," she said.

"It's going to be tough," Remy said. "I never could get one. The police refused to release any information, so over the years, I had to investigate in my own ways. I found a significant number of items, but nothing valuable, and none of them explained the ring's significance."

"But what if you never got the full list?" Jade turned to her partner. "Frank, get in touch with your San Francisco PD buddy."

Frank rose. "On my way."

While Frank made his call, Jade considered what Mo had learned. Coincidences? Maybe, but given Garner's planned appearance, she didn't think so. Had he learned the treasure—or whatever—was part of the original collection he owned? Did he need Remy to steal it back for him? He certainly needed Remy's key to get it.

And, most of all, what was *it?*

"Hey," David said, striding in from the other room. "What's for breakfast?"

Everybody ignored him.

Jade paced as she heard Frank mumbling into his cell phone on the other side of the room. Even if they found the piece, how would they know that was *it?* Could Remy really look at a list and tell what they were looking for?

"He's e-mailing the list," Frank said, flipping his phone closed and striding toward them.

Jade shook her head. "I'm not so sure—"

"And pictures," he added.

Mostly due to David's stomach growling and pitiful expression, Jade let him order room service while they waited for the e-mail. She ate nothing when the meal came thirty minutes later. She paced. "What the hell is taking so long?" she said, irritated by the delay. "Is he *drawing* the pictures?"

"It's a thirty-five-year-old theft, J.B.," Frank said, his gaze glued to the laptop screen.

David cut into his sausage links with enthusiasm. "It's amazing they have pictures of the stuff at all."

"Thanks for the encouragement," Jade said dryly.

"Quiet," Mo said to David.

"Hey, you get to be the big hero. Why can't I make a comment?" David asked.

"You wanna be the big hero, do something heroic," Mo said.

"You know, I'm an important part of this team, too. I—"

"Do you two mind fighting somewhere besides in front of our client?" Jade asked, crossing her arms over her chest and glaring at them.

Flushing, David glanced at Remy, who was smiling. "I nearly forgot. Sorry, boss."

Remy rose, slid his arm around Jade and urged her into his seat. She was too wound up. She needed to relax. And he could certainly think of a number of ways to make that happen. None of which involved this hotel suite he'd come to hate, or being surrounded by her wonderful, protective, but always present crew.

Would she be different if he got her alone? Would she feel differently toward him? Maybe not. Probably not. But he wanted to find out.

"Got 'em," Frank said.

They all rushed to the laptop, Jade, Mo and David standing back a bit, so he could get a clear look at the pictures. Frank pulled them up one by one so that they filled the screen. The resolution wasn't fantastic—evidence of somebody scanning print pictures into a digital file. There were three decent Impressionist-type paintings, a garish abstract and two plaster sculptures. All the work was done by three San Francisco artists, two of whom had made great strides in the last couple of decades. The collection Garner had stolen had actually risen in value.

If Remy didn't detest him, he might admire him.

"Not that I know what we're looking for exactly, but I don't see anything that connects to me. I've never owned or dealt with work by any of these artists, and I don't see how the ring—and its key—could unlock some mystery relating to them."

He could feel disappointment permeate the air. "Would it help to see them in person?" Frank asked.

"I don't see how. I'm not even sure what we're looking for."

"There's some connection here," Jade said. "I *know* it."

"I'll see if I can get the museum people to send us pictures of the collection they're showing," Mo said. "Maybe the police left off a piece, or maybe their pictures will be clearer. If I use Remy's name, I might even be able to get us an early, private tour."

"Sure. Why not?" Jade said, though with little confidence.

She, like him, obviously felt they had the final piece to the puzzle. They just didn't have the puzzle itself.

"Let's move on to the blueprints," she said.

She worked nonstop. She worked them all.

They ran through the layout of the gallery, the communication system, the roles each team member would play, the moves they anticipated Garner making, even the worst-case scenarios.

They got updates from Detective Parker—the most significant of which was that the waiter at Plush had picked Johnny Malden's cousin out of a lineup as the shooter at the restaurant. The San Francisco PD revealed that Garner was under investigation for several recent burglaries and were anxious to meet with Frank personally and pool information.

Now it seemed just a matter of trapping Garner and getting to the treasure before he did.

The case was spiraling to a conclusion, as was Remy's time with Jade.

She came to him each night, covering him with her touch and her kiss. She sought release. He gave it to her.

But it wasn't enough. It wasn't nearly enough.

THE DAY BEFORE the opening, Remy snagged her wrist as she rolled out of bed. "Let's go to the beach."

She shook her head.

He sat up. She wasn't blowing him off again. "This will be over tomorrow night."

Naked, beautiful and flushed in profile, she looked back. "Will it?"

"Yes."

He wanted to tell her that after this was over he wanted to still see her. But he didn't think she'd respond well to that news. He figured she'd respond even less enthusiastically to the news that he loved her. He wasn't sure exactly when it had happened or why, it just had.

Having her with him, beside him, had become essential. He wanted to know her better, spend more time with her. No matter their differences, he wanted to find a way to work them out.

He craved her smile and relished her touch. He valued her opinion and respected her talents.

She felt none of that for him, and he was running out of time.

"We can't do anything else for the operation today," he said. "We've planned, run through every scenario we can think of and followed up every lead. I need a break. *You* need a break. Just for one night."

"We can always do more," she said, but without much conviction.

"We can fly down to Florida this morning. My pilot's very trustworthy."

"Who's your pilot?"

"Me."

A hint of a smile touched her lips. "We're back here by ten tomorrow."

"Deal." He jerked her back into the bed and on top of him. "Pack light."

"I remember."

They escaped the suite with a surprising lack of commotion. Jade ordered all the guys to take twenty-four hours of R&R. They'd been in each other's company nonstop for almost a week, and the break was more than welcome.

On the way to the airport, Remy called a friend who owned a house in the tiny fishing village of Cedar Key, on the Gulf Coast of Florida. It was vacant at the moment, so he was cleared to borrow it for the day.

Jade said little during the trip down, and he let her have her space. They'd been part of each other's every thought and word the last few days, and he needed his own reflection time as much as she. He needed to plan something besides the operation against Garner. He needed a plan for hanging on to Jade.

He'd stolen a lot of things in his life, but never—at least to his knowledge—anyone's heart.

Would logic appeal to her?

Yes, he thought so. He had some good points to make there. Physical compatibility, check. Geographic compatibility, check. Even though they lived in different cities, he didn't have a problem moving to New Orleans. He could base his business anywhere. Friendship compatibility, check. They got along well most of the time and sensed each other's feelings and thoughts easily. Career compatibility, check plus.

Very few people in the world had the job experiences they did. Who else could he share his secrets with?

Future plans compatibility, big question mark. At least on his part. What was he going to do about the NSA? His boss was snooping around his life when he'd long since paid his dues, which grated. And he was tired of answering to jerks like Hillman.

Last, moral compatibility. Another question mark. He and Jade would have to talk this one out.

Exploring his thoughts on the matter, he came to one blatantly honest conclusion—though he'd given up his illegal activities and had no intention of going back, he didn't share her total black-and-white view of the world.

Could they compromise enough to make this relationship work?

The only goal he'd ever failed to meet was learning more about his father and the significance of the ring. He was about to finally complete that mission. With his past resolved, his future stretched out before him with new hope and expectation.

He wanted to share that future with Jade.

As he took the plane down for a landing, he vowed to dazzle her with food, wine and sex, then hit her hard with logical arguments and sincere confessions.

"Where's the runway?" she asked, peaking out her side window.

He nodded just ahead of them. "Right there."

"You're kidding."

Admittedly, it was a small strip with water at each end, but he wasn't exactly a novice pilot and his plane hadn't let him down yet. Though if it did, he supposed he wouldn't be around for regrets.

"Relax. We'll be down in less than five minutes."

"I guess so," she said doubtfully, "one way or another."

He set the plane down with practiced ease on the small runway. After he'd parked and unloaded their small bags, he led her toward the house, which was situated just a few hundred yards away.

Inhaling the tangy sea air, he felt a world away from Atlanta and the tension there. A golf cart—the preferred method of transportation in the area—was parked out front when they arrived at the house, which his friend had renovated to fit in with the simple beach community. He punched in the security code his friend had given him and let Jade precede him inside.

The house was secluded and private, with a fully equipped kitchen and an amazing view of the gulf. The tide was on its way out at the moment, so the oyster beds that littered the shoreline were revealed, jutting through the sparkling blue water.

He'd been there several times over the past couple of years. It was the perfect weekend getaway to escape the stress of his job and the bustling city where he lived.

"How about some lunch?" he asked as she stared through the windows at the water.

"I didn't see a takeout place on the way in. For that matter, I didn't see a grocery store or even another person. Did you take over the whole island?"

"No. It's just quiet here. Lunch?" He extended his arm toward the kitchen.

"You cook?"

"The basics, and I made a call to a local seafood market before we arrived. Everything we need should be here. Do you like clams?"

"Sure."

"They're a local specialty."

She sat on one of the barstools at the counter, and he went to work boiling spinach fettuccini, chopping onions and melting butter. He added garlic, lemon, white wine and fresh parsley to the sauce, and they were eating in minutes.

"This is great," she said. "I'm not much of a cook myself. I don't have the patience for it."

"You should try it more. It's relaxing."

During the meal, they talked about random, everyday things—the weather at the beach, the many types of birds that flew past the windows and fished in the water, movies they liked and hated, their favorites foods and restaurants. It was uplifting, going back to the beginning, where most couples start.

Once their plates were loaded into the dishwasher, he slipped his hand in hers and led her out the back door. On the deck were several lounge chairs. Unlike summer, when Florida was sticky and humid unless you were in the water, mid-February brought cool breezes that enabled you to be outside at any time of the day.

Saying nothing, he settled in one of the chairs and pulled her into his lap. She curled up, laid her head on his shoulder and sighed. He'd never seen her so passive, so easygoing. The measure of her relaxation was so great she'd even taken off her boots and shoulder holster.

His hands trembled as he held her. He loved her intense and vibrant, energetic and bossy. Seeing this side of her, his love for her deepened and strengthened.

After several minutes of listening to the water and watching the wildlife, she lifted her head. "Thank you."

"For?"

"Convincing me to come here. The pressure was getting

to me, but I didn't want to admit it." She pressed her lips lightly to his. "You're really okay sometimes."

"Don't get all gushy on me."

She rubbed the pad of her thumb over his bottom lip, and her gaze softened. "I might. You've been really strong throughout all this. You've cooperated and followed my lead without letting me completely take over. That's quite an admirable skill."

"Since you usually just run people over."

She laughed. "Usually." She sobered abruptly. "This trip back in time can't have been easy for you. Remembering the deaths of your friend and your mother again, going through the frustration of never knowing your father's identity or what his intentions were in giving you the ring. Have I helped, or driven you crazy?"

"You've been amazing."

"I'm glad. I want you to resolve your past. To be happy."

"This all sounds like a goodbye."

She looked down and away. "I guess it is in a way."

He scooped her in his arms and stood. "You're not getting rid of me just yet."

Carrying her inside to the bedroom, he laid her on the bed before pulling down the room-darkening shades, so that the only light came from the door that led to the deck. He foraged for candles, found several and placed them around the room, lighting them each in turn.

When he turned back to the bed, she was lying on her stomach, naked and watching him.

He frowned. "I was going to undress you myself."

Smiling, she stared up at him. "I can put them back on."

"I don't think that we need to be that drastic." He sat next to her and trailed his fingers down her bare, warm back. "You have beautiful skin."

She laid her head on the bed and stretched out her arms. "You can keep doing that forever."

The word *forever* made him hesitate a moment. She couldn't possibly mean that seriously, but given his train of thought earlier, it ridiculously gave him hope.

He slid the tips of his fingers, slowly, up and down her back. It was toned without being overly muscular. Her skin, glossy and smooth, smelled like—he leaned close to check—

"Lemons?"

She seemed to need no explanation. "Do you have any idea how hard it is to find a lotion that doesn't smell like somebody's flower garden exploded in your bathroom?"

No, he supposed he didn't.

Shrugging, he strengthened the pressure, pressing his fingers, then the heels of his hands into her lower back. Applying rolling pressure, he moved up her spine before he gripped her shoulders and kneaded them between his thumb and fingers. Though certainly not a massage therapist, even he could feel the tension in her neck and at the base of her skull.

He worked all those muscles gently, then with increasingly firm pressure as they continued to loosen. Concentrating so completely on her, he was surprised to find himself growing warm, not just from the sensual act of touching her but because he'd been putting so much strength and effort into working her tight muscles.

I could give up the NSA and go to massage therapy school.

When she'd relaxed so far into the mattress that she was in danger of slipping through to the floor, he changed his pace, smoothing his fingertips over her skin. Drawing his touch from side to side, then up and down.

"Mmm," she said, rolling over. Her eyes were closed. "Taking your time is such a luxury."

His gaze locked on her breasts. His body hardened. He was ready to move his massage to the front.

But she sat up so quickly they nearly bumped heads. "Your turn."

She unbuttoned his shirt and tossed it on the floor, then urged him onto his stomach. When she straddled him, the damp center of her body pressed against his lower back, he groaned.

"It only gets better from here," she said in his ear, her breath hot on the back of his neck.

He closed his eyes, wondering if he could take anything better.

13

JADE SMOOTHED HER palms over Remy's back, loving the heat and ripple of muscle beneath her hands. No matter how many times she saw his body, she continued to be fascinated.

The breadth of his chest made her sigh in feminine appreciation. The warmth of his skin made her long to touch him, to run her fingers along every curve and plane, to feel the muscles tighten in longing.

Would she ever grow tired of his touch? Of him touching her? It didn't matter. She didn't have a choice. He'd be gone soon.

Her accountant would handle settling his bill, and Remington Tremaine would move on to smile seductively at someone else. To another blonde. Or at least a woman of equal sophistication who understood his love of art. Who didn't carry a gun, or stay up all night as part of a surveillance team. Who was normal and giving. Who wanted to share things with him, instead of holding herself apart.

But one who didn't know *him.* You *know him like no one else*.

Part of her actually believed that. She appreciated his sense of adventure and excitement. She sensed when he was giving her a crock of bull. She understood when he was in pain and trying to hide it. She empathized with his frustration and anger at the NSA.

But there were many aspects of him she didn't get at all—

his tendency to see a hard-and-fast rule as merely an obstacle to move around or go over, the way he shrugged off injustice, and his motivations for stealing what he wanted instead of using that clever brain of his to succeed legitimately.

She shook her head. Today was about relaxation and enjoyment. It was a moment out of time she'd probably look back on years from now. A moment when she'd touched someone amazing, when she'd been wanted for something more than just her attitude and marksman skills.

Once she'd reduced his muscles to jelly, just as he had hers, she stretched on top of him—her naked front to his naked back. She laid her arms and hands over his, curling her fingers to join them. She kissed his earlobe, which happened to be the only part she could reach without moving.

"Make love with me?" she asked, comfy and sleepy, but knowing he could rouse her if he chose.

He released her hands briefly and rolled them both to their sides. Now, she could see his face in the flickering candlelight that danced across his strong cheekbones. His eyes were dark and serious. He wrapped his arms around her waist.

"Anytime you want," he said, his voice husky.

His expression, his words, made her catch her breath. What was happening here? What did this really mean? Why didn't this feel like a release from the tension of the case or a fun affair all of a sudden?

She swallowed her anxiety. She was imagining things. She was *too* relaxed, if that was possible.

She kissed his jaw. "Now's good." She slid her hand over his shoulder and down his back. "Touch me, Remy. I need you to touch me."

He cupped her backside and pulled her against him, his

erection nudging her hip. As he covered her mouth with his, she flung her leg over his waist, so that her aching center could feel the hard ridge of his cock.

She groaned as a ripple of pleasure rolled up her spine. The material of his pants created both friction and frustration. She wanted him naked against her, but she enjoyed cranking up the hunger. He kissed her deeply, his hand gripping the back of her head to angle her just the way he wanted. His intense need was palpable.

He pushed his hips against hers. She bumped him back.

He trailed his lips across her shoulder. His breath was heaving. "I need to be inside you."

When he started to unbuckle his belt, she shifted her weight and rolled him to his back. Even as she unbuttoned his pants, he rolled his hips. She followed his rhythm mindlessly, knowing she could end the torture if she just got his clothes off, but there was a lovely kind of dance, a sinuous rhythm to their movements.

When she finally stopped moving long enough to part him from the rest of his clothes, she wasted no time in grabbing one of the condoms he'd laid on the bedside table and rolling it over his erection. She raised herself above him, and he gripped her hips to guide her. She leaned down to kiss him one last time, then plunged, driving him deep inside her body.

She arched her back, stretching to take every last bit of him and pushing her clitoris against the base of his penis. Desire vibrated from her center to her toes, then back up again. Her belly trembled.

Bracing her palms on his stomach and closing her eyes to fully appreciate every sensation, she shifted her hips. He moved with her, his breath coming in short pants, his hands clenching her hips.

Their movements rapidly became shorter and harder. She braced her hands on the mattress to better pump her hips. He bent his knees, changed the angle of penetration and she gasped.

The spiral of need tightened to the point she thought she'd snap in half like a rubber band. She needed that pop. She chased the elusive blast of pleasure, and, mercifully, it finally crashed over her, milking every last impulse and sensation she had, draining her of energy, contracting her heart and leaving her to wonder how she'd ever take another step knowing she was losing him.

Soon. And forever.

JADE NAPPED ON Remy's chest, listening vaguely to the lap of the water against the shore and feeling the ocean breeze through the windows they'd opened. This slice of heaven might evaporate in moments, but she was soaking it all up in the meantime.

When they finally slid out of bed, he made more clams—this time with fresh herbs, chopped tomatoes and spicy sausage over rice—then they watched a DVD.

"How did you and Mo meet?" he asked as they slouched on the sofa and watched the sun set behind the house in beautiful shades of pink and purple.

"His father was head of security at Beau's. He took over about the time I went to Tulane. When my parents were killed, he was my lifeline. I don't know what I would have done without him. He watched Beau's for me and made sure I had something to come home to." She slid her fingers over the back of his hand, thinking of all she owed Mo. "He was the only person I told about the NSA—even though I wasn't supposed to tell anybody."

"*You* broke a rule?" he asked, his voice light and teasing.

"I've stepped outside the lines once or twice. I simply don't see the point in doing so just for the sake of rebelling." She lifted her chin, knowing she sounded stiff, but also knowing they'd never agree on this point. "My parents raised me to be a productive member of society."

"I was raised by nuns. A strong moral base isn't always a guarantee of following the straight and narrow."

"So why didn't you?"

"I was always drawn to excitement and risk."

"I hear the police academy is always looking for candidates."

"Too traditional. I'm a rebel." He gripped her hand. "Do you think I'm proud of my thievery?"

"You certainly don't apologize for it."

"No, because sometimes it was justified, and in many ways it helped me become a better person."

She turned over to face him. "You've *got* to be kidding."

"I'm not kidding. But that doesn't mean I don't regret many of my actions. I've grown into a different person than the boy who snuck out of the orphanage for kicks. Between then and now, I've had too many scary moments. I've seen too much of the dark side of life." He lifted her chin so she met his gaze. "Contrary to rumor, I have a conscience."

"I never said—"

He laid his finger over her lips. "Sister Mary Katherine always assured me I had conscience in abundance. Eventually, it wouldn't let me escape the simple fact that what I was doing was wrong. It wasn't challenging, or amusing or satisfying. It was *wrong*."

Her throat tightened. She'd never realized he felt this way. She'd assumed his friend's death, followed by his going to the police, had *forced* him to give up his illegal activities.

Seeming to read her thoughts, he smoothed back her hair. "Maybe we're not as far apart as you think."

How did that change what was between them? She was tempted to pass off the moment as nothing more than temporary lover chitchat, where the closeness is forced and artificial. But that was only because she was afraid if she examined her feelings for him, she might find a great deal more than she was willing to give in to.

"But my feelings about my past are in conflict now," he continued. "On this side of the law, do I have a right to judge Peter Garner so harshly?"

"Yes." Hell, surely he wasn't comparing himself to Garner. "You're *not* him. He's cruel and heartless. He's responsible for the death of one man we know about and no telling how many others. He has no loyalty or compassion." She lay her hands against his chest. "You have a heart. A generous heart. You're protective of your friends. You're strong without making others look weak. I—" she looked away, then back "—I admire you for what you've done with your life."

He pulled her close, kissing her neck. "You have no idea how much I've needed to hear that."

"Not that I agree with all your choices."

He chuckled. "I wouldn't expect you to."

She pulled back slightly. "Are we going to be friends after all this?"

"I hope so."

"You know, I thought you were an arrogant manipulator when I first met you."

"I thought you were a control freak."

"I am," she said.

"You're tough. But amazing."

"You're difficult. But brilliant."

He leaned close to her lips. "Let's admire each other in bed."

Jade briefly gave herself over to his touch and kiss, but before she let him lead her to the bedroom, she checked in with her team. Frank was having dinner with a former colleague. Mo had gone to the movies earlier and was Internet-surfing again. David seemed to be in a loud nightclub, possibly one where women took off their clothes for money.

At least they were separated and doing what they wanted for a change.

Jade focused on Remy. She reveled in his touch and his smile, in the pleasure he gave her, in the way he sighed against her body. She didn't even consider tomorrow and the focus she'd have to regain. She refused to let her mind wander to the future, when the case was over and he would be gone.

They talked little as they flew back the next morning. Holding hands communicated their silent regret at having to return.

"I want to continue to see you after the case is over," he said in the limo on the way back to the hotel.

Startled, she looked over at him. "You live here, I live in New Orleans."

"I have a plane, remember? Besides, I'm leaving the NSA, so my schedule will be much more flexible."

Obviously the break had dulled her senses. "Leaving the NSA?"

"I've had enough. When you've lost all trust and respect for your boss, it's time to give notice."

"I guess so."

She threaded her fingers through her hair. Did she want

to see him? *Should* she see him? Her emotions were jumbled and incoherent. She enjoyed him, but could they really have a *relationship?*

How long could they really expect to make it?

Now wasn't the time to be talking about this. She had to put her personal feelings aside, lock them in a box. She had to find the kick-ass bodyguard. Fast. "You seem to be making some rash decisions this morning," she said, not knowing what else to say.

"I've been thinking about them for a while."

"A week." She rolled the tension from her shoulders. "Let's get through tonight. We need to concentrate on that."

"Don't push me aside, Jade," he said, his tone edgy.

"I'm not. I just—" Leaning forward, she rubbed her temples with the tips of her fingers. "I don't know what I want—except to get that son of a bitch Garner. I didn't plan on you, on feeling…close to you. Me, who plans everything. I didn't anticipate that very big potential problem."

"I didn't, either." He sighed. "I'm sorry for unloading this on you now. It'll keep." He grabbed her hand and pulled her against his chest. "Do your job. I'll do mine." Kissing her, he murmured against her lips, "We'll meet in the middle."

She curled her hand around his neck, knowing their privacy was ending, praying she could be strong enough, quick enough, smart enough to pull them out of this one. The world without Remy—or any man on her team—wasn't a place she was willing to be. "You've got a deal."

They kept their hands clasped until the elevator doors opened on the eighteenth floor, where they broke apart. Jade checked the clip on her pistol. Remy smoothed the cuffs on his shirt. Then they walked, side-by-side, back into the fray.

"HEY, BOSS, REMY," Mo said as they walked through the suite's doorway.

Remy noted Mo's always-serious expression was brighter. David also greeted them with renewed enthusiasm. Frank was taking a phone call in the other room and waved through the connecting door.

Even though he'd taken her away for mostly selfish reasons, Remy was pleased to see the team had responded well to the break. Tonight was about much more than his life. Frank, Mo, David and Jade were all risking their lives for *him*. Yes, that was their job, but it didn't make their commitment and potential sacrifice any less moving.

"I got the digital pictures from the museum," Mo said. "A bunch of pieces aren't on the list of what Garner and Nagel supposedly stole. There are donations from other collectors—the works being shown feature San Francisco artists, which was probably why his pieces were included."

"Let's see them," Jade said, heading toward the laptop on the dining room table.

Remy followed, though he didn't know what he expected to find. How would he recognize a significant piece? He owned a few works by San Francisco artists. Was this about one of them?

He leaned over Mo's shoulder and watched him click through the pictures they'd already seen. Thirty-five years had passed. Even if they could prove Garner was involved in the robbery, the statute of limitations had long run out. No one—including him—had definitively connected him to Nagel's murder until now. What evidence could they possibly pull together now?

He watched the pictures of paintings, then a series of sculptures flash on the screen.

"Wait," he said, leaning closer to stare at a bronze sculpture. He could feel the blood drain from his face. "That's my mother."

Jade gripped the back of Mo's chair. "What?"

"That sculpture—the face, the hair. She looks like my mother."

"What does this mean?" Jade asked, her eyes wide. "Did your mother know Garner?"

"I don't know," he said. "Maybe. If Nagel is my father, then it's even more likely they'd met at some point."

"Where did it come from, Mo? Garner's collection?"

Mo enlarged the section at the bottom, where the caption was printed. "State of California."

"Probably a repossession from an estate," Remy said, curling his fist around the ring in his pocket. "The owner died without a will or living relatives."

"How did it wind up in a show with Garner's stuff?" David asked, though of course no one knew.

Jade paced away, then back. "This is wild. Are you sure?"

"It's a bronze, as in *Remington* bronze, and it looks just like my mother." Remy's heart was pounding. The resemblance was astounding. He only had a couple of pictures of his mother— the ones she'd left with the nuns when she'd dropped him off at the orphanage. Long, silky-looking dark hair, dark eyes, short, upturned nose. The features were the same on the bronze.

Had she been a model?

Had his father seen the statue somewhere and noticed the similarity to the mother of his child? Had he stolen it for himself, rather than Garner, as Remy had always suspected?

Was it possible his mother actually posed for the sculpture, or was the resemblance just a coincidence?

He knew one thing for sure—he had to have that statue. Remy would bet everything he had that the key in his pocket fit somewhere in it.

"Forget the gallery showing," he said. "We have to get that sculpture."

"We will," Jade said. "Is there any way to change the angle on that picture, Mo?"

"No. There are just the brochure shots."

"We need to call Detective Parker and get him to confiscate the piece."

"No." Remy shook his head. "Absolutely not. We're not bringing in the cops. I can get it without them."

Jade crossed her arms over her chest. "Can you?"

He met her gaze and refused to flinch at the judgment in her eyes. "Yes, I can. With or without your help."

Mo and David grew still, obviously sensing the tension.

Frank walked into the room. "So, what's—"

Remy was aware of his stare, but he didn't look away from Jade. As Mo explained the new development, Remy cursed silently. He should have known she wouldn't understand. She was too stringent, too inflexible. He'd hoped, after yesterday—

He broke off the thought. Maybe, if he hadn't been presented with this temptation, they could have found a compromise, but now he knew that wasn't possible.

He *had* to have that sculpture, and he was getting it the only way he knew how. Anxious energy flowed through him. "You guys go to the showing and distract Garner. I'll get the sculpture."

"*Get?* You mean *steal*." Jade grabbed his arm. "No, the police can—"

"*No police,*" he said, glaring at her. He'd involved the police once. He wouldn't go to them for help again. Not even for Jade.

"J.B.," Frank said quietly as he approached them. "I've got to agree with Remy. Let's not get Parker involved." He stepped closer when she shook her head. "The police will haul Garner in for questioning, he won't give them anything, then they'll take the sculpture and stuff it in some evidence room, and we'll never know what's going on. Let's handle it ourselves, not tip our hand to Garner, then the cops can take the credit for the bust."

"Unless they bust *him*," she said, nodding her head at Remy.

Remy clenched his jaw.

"They won't," Frank said. "I say we go to the gallery opening, get what we can from Garner, then go to the museum first thing in the morning and make an offer on the sculpture. Museums always need money, and everybody's happy."

"Garner will get it," Remy said, shaking his head. "He's going to the show as a cover, while his team breaks into the museum and gets the sculpture."

"I don't think so," Mo said. "The thing came from San Francisco. If he knew what he was looking for and where to find it, why come out here?"

"I'm with Mo," David said. "He could have ripped it off or bought it from a state auction at any time."

Frank nodded. "He doesn't know what he's looking for, and he needs you and that key to find it."

"That's why your father left you the key," Jade said slowly, "because he knew you would recognize the sculpture of your mother and find whatever's hidden inside it. He may have helped steal it, but he wanted you, *not Garner,* to have it."

His heart racing, Remy squeezed his eyes shut. They were making way too much sense.

A lifetime of mystery, of wondering if cold-eyed Sean Nagel, the lousy, small-time thief was his father, of searching for some meaning in his father's gift. It was all coming to fruition. It was nearly impossible to think clearly and reason through the most sensible plan.

"You're right," he said finally, ashamed that his first instinct had been to take the piece of art instead of buy it. "I'm sorry, I—"

A jolt of electricity shot through him. Cold sweat rolled down his face. What was happening to him? He was losing it.

"David," Jade said, laying her hand on his shoulder. "Get Remy a glass of whiskey."

"It's barely ten o'clock in the morning."

"Just get it."

She steered Remy toward the sofa. "Sit."

Surprised to feel light-headed, Remy did as she said.

She sat next to him, laying her hand on his thigh. Once David had poured the drink, she pushed the crystal against his palm. "Drink."

He did, welcoming the burn of liquor down his throat. Maybe it would knock him out of this weird, contrasting state of numb anxiousness.

"Better?" she asked.

He nodded slowly, his gaze sliding to hers. "Thanks."

"Least you didn't pass out," David said jovially, rapping him on the shoulder.

"Why would I—"

"Shock," Jade said quietly. "You're in shock."

Humiliation rolled over him. He'd been in dozens of tight situations before and had never fallen apart. What was wrong with him?

"It's harder when it's personal," Jade said, squeezing his thigh.

"After J.B. shot that punk who killed her parents, she dropped to the floor and cried," Frank added, sounding proud.

Jade rolled her eyes. "Gee, Frank, thanks for helping us all relive that fabulously brave moment."

Her dry comment shook Remy from his embarrassment, and he managed a smile.

"Enough slacking," Jade said as she rose. "Time to work."

She checked weapons and surveillance equipment. She went over blueprints with a magnifying glass. She drilled them on their roles. She examined everyone's wardrobe and tracking devices. She went over every picture and every scrap of information they'd gathered about Peter Garner.

Finally, she let everyone separate to go to their own rooms, get dressed and gather their thoughts.

Remy showered and dressed quickly. He tried not to think about the night ahead. He'd never been so apprehensive and so excited about an operation. Jade was right. It was different when it was personal.

When the knock came, he wasn't surprised to open the door and find Jade on the other side.

Her gaze was hesitant. "Can I come in?"

He extended his arm. "Sure."

When the door was closed behind her, she leaned back against it. And, either he was emotional or overly tuned to her, but the moment reminded him of the first night they'd been together. She'd come to him in physical need. He thought they'd moved on to something more.

But he wasn't so sure now. He loved her. He wanted to tell her, but he was afraid she'd turn away from him.

She walked toward him and slid her arms around his neck. "Hang in there, Tremaine. We've got your back."

He didn't have to explain. She understood the emotions pressing on him, the sensation of hanging on the edge, of a huge change in his life just over the horizon. He shouldn't have doubted her.

"I'm a second-generation thief," he said against her cheek.

"I suppose so."

"You and I, we may be different, but we have a bond, don't we?"

"Yes."

"I need you now, Jade. I'm a mess."

"I know. That's why I'm here."

She kissed his throat and pressed her chest against his. Her warmth infused him with strength and energy. Her body pleasured him, gave him release and reminded him of the possibilities of the future.

As they lay together on the bed, he fought to find a balance. He tried to remember why he was here, what had brought him to this point, but Jade kissed his shoulder and rolled out of bed. The distraction of her body kept his mind occupied until she returned moments later, dressed in a black satin bra and matching skimpy panties.

"Why do my disguises always require a push-up bra and heels?"

Licking his lips, he ran his gaze down her body—her mostly bare body. "You'd rather Mo wear them?"

"I'd rather wear jeans and a T-shirt."

"As long as you cover up somehow. I'll never be able to concentrate on the operation otherwise."

She did, wearing black silky pants and a low-cut green blouse that matched her eyes. The pants were strategic, of course, since she needed something to hide the small pistol she strapped to her calf. She wore her hair up, exposing sparkling chandelier-style earrings that also served as a transmitter.

She deserved to be taken to a classy jazz club or elegant dinner, not into the company of a viper like Peter Garner.

"Thank you," he said when he, Jade and Mo were in the limo, knowing Frank, following in a van, could also hear him. "All of you."

"We're not done yet," Jade said.

"But we're going to be moving at 180 miles an hour in a few minutes. I didn't want my appreciation to go unsaid."

"Wait 'til my accountant sends you the bill," she said. "Then show your appreciation."

Remy smiled along with Mo, and before they said another word, the limo had stopped at the front door of the gallery. He straightened the cuffs on his shirt and waited for Charlie to open the door.

As he escorted Jade through the front door, a sense of calm rolled though him. After all the preparation and anticipation, he'd arrived at a moment of truth in his life. He slid his hand over the hidden pocket in his pants in which he'd sewn the ring. One way or another, with or without answers from Garner, he'd finally know what the gift from his father meant.

A waiter presented him and Jade with a tray of champagne when they walked into the main room of the gallery. The two-story room was dominated by smooth white walls and a chrome walkway that encircled the octagonal room on the second floor. People, mostly dressed in black, wandered around, pretending to look at the paintings on the walls, though their main focus seemed to be checking each other out.

He wasn't sure if it was Jade's striking coloring or Mo's fierce expression, but they certainly got their share of stares.

"I thought people came to look at paintings," Jade whispered to him.

"They're just props," Remy said.

They wandered around, and Remy spoke to a couple of people he knew. He explained Mo's presence as his bodyguard, and they were all shocked to learn he'd been shot.

Garner was nowhere in sight, but he'd anticipated the man would be late to make a grand entrance. It gave him and Jade the opportunity to look at the room in actuality, rather than just on the paper they'd been studying the last few days.

David, dressed in a waiter's uniform, walked by them a few times. Frank was in place in the surveillance van, and they didn't have to worry about Lucas and Vanessa popping in, since she had a big catering job that night and had convinced Lucas she couldn't do it without his help. Remy was grateful. Jade would have had a hard time concentrating if she had to worry about Lucas, too.

So, the gang's all here. Save one.

Forty-five minutes after they arrived, he walked through the door. Alone, with little fanfare, though several people recognized him, sending whispers through the room. Blond and tanned, dressed in an expensive, dark-blue designer suit, he looked the same as he had the last time Remy had seen him. He certainly didn't look the sixty-plus years he must be.

But then he'd probably sold his soul to the devil a long time ago, and would no doubt never age normally.

Jade squeezed his arm, letting him know she recognized their prey.

They stayed put and watched him. He worked his way slowly toward them, in a very slick, unobvious way.

"How nice to see you again, Mr. Tremaine," he said, shaking Remy's hand when he finally reached them. "It's been a number of years, hasn't it?"

"Yes, it has," Remy said, forcing himself to relax his grip on his glass.

"Well, I guess we have a lot to talk about then. How about joining me for a private meeting? I believe there's a conference room open on the second floor."

14

JADE COULD HARDLY believe the ease with which she, Remy and Mo had gotten Garner alone.

And the very ease—plus the fact that *he'd* made the suggestion—immediately made her suspicious and edgy. Though she wanted to stand, she accepted the chair Remy pulled out for her.

Introductions were made all around, and Jade saw a gleam of pride appear in Garner's eyes when Mo was introduced as Remy's security guard. He stood by the door, a silent sentry that allowed her to focus on Garner.

"Yes, I heard you ran into a bit of trouble last week," he said with a slight smile. "Twice, I believe."

"Did you?" Remy said coolly as he settled into his chair.

Though Remy had mentioned the restaurant shooting to some of the guests earlier, he hadn't said anything about a second attack. Garner was practically admitting he'd instigated Remy's *trouble,* and the casual confession set Jade's nerves further on edge.

"Atlanta is a dangerous city," Garner said, his gaze fixed on Remy.

"It certainly can be."

"There have been a number of new developments in the art world since we last spoke, Mr. Tremaine. I'd like to share them with you and perhaps you can help me out with a little problem I have."

It couldn't be this easy. Jade kept her eyes focused on Garner, but her ears tuned to the other side of the door. When would ten hired goons burst in and force them all to some secret location where they'd be tortured and questioned?

"Fine," Remy said, nodding.

"I recently came into possession of a very interesting letter," Garner began. "An old colleague of mine, who died many years ago—actually, you'll recognize his name, Mr. Tremaine." He smiled slightly. "It's Sean Nagel."

Remy nodded and said nothing.

Jade tried to breathe normally. Remy's father? Would they finally know the truth? Did Garner even know?

"Well, Nagel's cousin passed away a few weeks ago. When she did, her attorney contacted me because he had discovered an envelope in her safety deposit box with my name on it. Inside was a letter from Nagel that told an illuminating story of a betrayal I'd long suspected, but had never been able to prove.

"Many years ago, Nagel had *acquired* some private collection items for me, one of them rumored to be a van Gogh overpaint."

Remy's eyebrows lifted with obvious skepticism. "A missing van Gogh?"

"Yes, the odds seemed long to me, as well. However, when the items arrived, the piece wasn't among them. Mr. Nagel said it wasn't there. I was displeased, but it had just been a rumor, so I wasn't overly disappointed.

"Many years went by—at least fifteen—and Mr. Nagel and I continued to do business together occasionally. Then another piece he was supposed to acquire for me came up missing. When I communicated my displeasure—" no doubt threatening his life "—Mr. Nagel admitted he'd betrayed me with the van Gogh overpaint. He promised to turn over both missing pieces immediately. Remember, I hadn't told him *why* that particular painting was important fifteen years ago, just that I wanted it. Unfortunately, he couldn't reacquire the overpaint, so I washed my hands of him."

"You killed him," Remy said.

Garner shrugged. "I know he died. How, I couldn't say."

"Killing him was a huge mistake."

"Well, given what I've recently learned, his absence has certainly made things more difficult. For one, I felt the need to donate several of the items I'd acquired and sent to the High Museum, far from my West Coast shores. Of course, if their theft was ever investigated, I had bills of sale from Sean Nagel. How could I ever imagine he'd sold me stolen goods?" He smiled slightly. "It pays to be cautious."

"How does this apply to me?" Remy asked.

"Years after Nagel's death, who should appear but a man following his path. You." Again, Garner smiled. "His son, who seemed not to have fallen far from the light-fingered tree—or so I assumed—looking for the trail of his dead father."

Seemed? Assumed?

Jade tried to keep her expression neutral. Did Garner not know for certain if Nagel was Remy's father? Maybe he was just as in the dark as they were.

Calm and elegant, Garner crossed one foot over his knee. "I wasn't concerned with you at the time. Then the letter from the attorney arrived, and I realized how much Nagel's incompetence had cost me. The letter was a documentation—or maybe a confession—of his contact with my overpaint."

My overpaint, Jade thought in disgust. The one he'd *stolen* from somebody else.

"After taking the overpaint, Nagel tried researching it, so he could learn its value and sell it. But he couldn't find the work in any art book or anywhere in the library. He'd concluded it was worthless, given it to a local artist friend and considered the matter closed."

Jade couldn't help it, she gawked. "He'd *given it away?*"

"Apparently, but when I demanded he get it back, he went to see the local artist—who had some talent but usually flushed away his funds on wine and poker games. When Nagel asked for the painting, the artist just laughed.

"He'd been clever enough to see the work was an overpaint, and though he had no idea what it obscured, he'd decided it would only be more valuable as the years went by." Garner's eyes, though cold until now, lit from within. "So he'd concealed it in a bronze statue he'd made, then created a key in the form of an onyx ring and given it to his son."

Dear God. Jade laid her hand over Remy's. She could feel the tension in his body.

"My father was the artist," he said.

"Yes." His smile was cruel. "Paul O'Brian told Nagel he'd stored the sculpture in a warehouse he rented, probably never dreaming his friend would want the piece so badly he'd kill for it."

The casual way he told Remy his father's name and about his murder made Jade want to jump over the table and punch that smarmy, composed smile off his face. If it was the last thing she ever did, she was going to kick his ass.

"Nor could Nagel have anticipated being unable to find the sculpture in the warehouse, or how difficult it would be to get the ring. Mr. Tremaine, you were fifteen at this time, so I imagine you've known this part of the story much longer than I have."

"Nagel came to see me."

"And didn't succeed in getting the all-important key. Realizing he'd failed, I'm assuming he chose to write down his journey as protection for himself should anything ever happen to him. Or maybe he wanted to piss me off from his grave. But either his cousin didn't care about the letter he gave her, or she forgot, because it sat in her safety deposit box until her recent death."

"So what happened to the sculpture?" Jade asked. How had the state come to own it?

"It was in O'Brian's basement all along. That idiot Nagel hadn't even bothered to search the house for it." Garner's eyes gleamed as he stared at Remy. "Your father, who had no will or living family members anybody knew about, lost his assets to the State of California. But his work will go on display tomorrow at the High Museum of Art, along with my collection, as part of a special tribute to San Francisco designers."

Remy had been right. The bronze sculpture was meant for him. But his father hadn't *stolen* it, he'd *created* it. And by making it in the image of Remy's mother, he'd been sure his son would be the only person who'd be interested in finding it.

He'd tried to secure his son's future by hiding a painting by Vincent van Gogh in one of his own works. It was beyond incredible.

"So, you can see my problem," Garner continued in the same cool tone. "I need you to find this bronze sculpture— there are quite a few in the collection—and I need you to unlock it with your special key, so that I can get my painting."

His arrogance was unbelievable. He couldn't honestly expect

that Remy was going to help him, could he? Was he going to offer him money? To split the profits of the van Gogh sale?

Remy's jaw clenched, then he said, "Why would I want to do that?"

Garner folded his hands on the table in front of him. "Because if you don't, I'm going to kill the man outside the gallery in the surveillance van."

Everything inside Jade went cold and still. Frank? Garner had Frank?

She shook her head. No. No, it wasn't possible.

"Boss?" Mo asked quietly from behind her.

"Stay here, please," she said, somehow managing to gather her thoughts. She pressed the panic button on her bracelet and seconds later David burst into the room. "The van," she said, rising. "Go check on Frank in the van."

As David rushed out, Garner commented, "I wondered whether you were really the girlfriend or part of the security detail. Johnny Malden's story of a foxy redhead knocking him to the ground seemed a bit fantastic to me. But it looks like that little mystery is cleared up."

Jade grabbed him by his tie and jerked him to his feet. "Where's Frank, you crazy bastard?"

He seemed startled by her show of force—and probably her strength. After all the bombshells he'd dropped, she was pleased she'd managed to throw him off stride.

"Threatening me will do you no good," he said, his voice strained from the pressure she was putting on his throat. "If I don't show up at my car in thirty minutes, my driver has instructions to radio my team, and they will kill your colleague."

Jade shoved him back in the chair and turned away. She faced Remy, whose fists were clenched at his sides. His eyes were full of fury and hatred as he stared at Garner. "How do we know he's still alive?"

"I can arrange for you to talk to him," Garner said.

"Do it." Remy glanced at her. "What do you need from me?"

"You get your wish." She swallowed. Her moral code, her sense of what was right and what was wrong, meant nothing against the leverage of Frank's life. "We'll get the sculpture—your way."

His eyes turned bleak for a moment, then he nodded. When Garner extended a cell phone toward him, he snatched it from his hand, then placed it in hers.

"Frank?" she said, fighting to keep her voice calm and professional.

"Hey, J.B. A couple of goons got the jump on the old man. Don't spread it around, okay?"

She thought of the way he'd unselfishly volunteered to let himself fall into Garner's clutches, of the sacrifices he'd made for her almost every day for the last thirteen years. "Hang in there. We're coming to get you."

"Figured you would."

"We'll give Garner what he wants, then we'll get you. Don't worry."

He laughed weakly. "Yeah, sure."

The line went dead, and Jade tossed Garner's phone back to him. She was afraid to get too close to him, since she was positive she'd strangle him.

She considered pulling out her pistol and forcing Garner to call his team back. She could bluff him. *You kill mine, I'll kill yours.* But she couldn't take the chance that Garner's goons would be as loyal to him as she was to Frank. She couldn't risk losing him.

"Frank's gone, J.B.," David said, panting as he raced into the room.

"The van and equipment?" she asked.

"Intact."

Well, well, their van Gogh lover wasn't nearly as clever as he thought. Jade very nearly smiled, and her heart settled back into its proper place in her chest.

The idiot had no idea that the balance of power had just shifted—unless he planned to have his people kill Frank the moment after she'd talked to him, but she didn't think so. He liked to stay far above the violence committed in his name.

And his side of the plan wasn't foolproof, either. What if Remy couldn't have cared less about Frank's life? As ruthless as Garner was, he counted on them to be honorable. It was remarkably flawed reasoning.

"Let's hear it, Garner," she said, glaring at him.

"When the painting's in my hand, you'll get your colleague back. You have three hours. That should give Mr. Tremaine enough time to get into the museum. I don't care whether you buy it, steal it or bribe your way to it. But I want it back here to make the exchange."

Jade shook her head. "Someplace more public. The bar in the lobby of the Marriott Marquis."

He was either really crazy or desperate because he nodded. "Fine."

But she knew he wasn't planning to kill her, Remy and her entire team on the spot. He'd be more likely to take his prize painting back to San Francisco, wait a month or two, then pay for a hit on Remy—this time with somebody who knew what they were doing. He would, no doubt, sell his van Gogh and retire anonymously on some tropical island, unconcerned whether Jade sent the cops or Feds chasing after him. He probably had a new identity already set up. The way he'd so boldly confronted them proved he thought he had a foolproof backup plan.

He didn't know Jade, though, and she had backup plans of her own. Peter Garner had messed with the wrong chick.

"Let's go." She spun without sparing Garner another glance and stalked from the room, Remy, Mo and David just behind her.

"I'm suddenly seeing the paranoid wisdom of putting a tracking device on every person on the team," Remy said as they raced down the stairs.

"You hired the best," Jade said simply.

HIS FATHER wasn't a thief.

He was a creator, not a taker.

The oddest sense of relief washed over Remy as he grabbed Jade's hand and they strode down the alley beside the museum. "The ventilation system is usually the best way, but let's check the security of the basement first."

"I say we walk up to the guard, hit him with pepper spray, then shoot anybody who comes after him."

"You're awfully aggressive tonight."

"I didn't get to beat the crap out of Garner. I'm edgy."

"Me, too, but if one of the guards manages to trip the alarm, the museum's security system will lock down—with us trapped inside it. I'd rather not chat with the FBI tonight, if you don't mind."

"Picky, picky."

They'd returned to the hotel long enough to grab supplies and change clothes. In traditional second-story-man style they'd both dressed in all black.

The team had scattered, with Charlie and the limo driving around the blocks surrounding the museum, ready to be their getaway car. David and Mo were following Frank's homing beacon in the van. Jade had instructed them to keep watch and go in after him only if Garner's hired goons made any homicidal moves.

They intended to meet him with the painting, after all. They just planned to bring the police—extras that Garner definitely wouldn't want to see. Between the goons who'd taken Frank, Johnny Malden, the ongoing investigation at the San Francisco PD and the publicity a van Gogh was bound to generate, they were confident a case could finally be brought against Garner.

If not, Remy and Jade had vowed to dog his steps until he made a mistake they could nail him for.

The pain he was putting her through, and the choice she'd had to make to save Frank, weighed heavily on his mind.

"Stop stalling," Jade said, tugging on his hand.

Unaware of how much he'd slowed his pace while lost in thought, he shook off the distractions and focused on the area around him.

Except for their footsteps and the occasional passing of a car on the main road, he heard nothing. Security cameras were pointed toward the front and back entrances, but not in the alley.

After studying the security layout Jade had retrieved after a desperate phone call to a fellow investigative firm, Remy was nearly positive the tiny basement windows that faced the alley were not wired to the alarm. All the storage areas were locked and wired with motion sensors, and, of course, the door into the main building was wired, as well, so getting into the basement really wouldn't get them very far.

Though certainly out of practice, Remy was pretty sure he could handle the doors. It was the cameras and motion detectors in the main exhibition areas that would be the real trick. Their plan was for him to go to the van Gogh display, set off the motion sensor, then turn off the camera. When the guards came to investigate, Jade was going to get the bronze they'd come for. The works in that area weren't valuable enough to warrant motion detectors.

It was primitive, but with the time frame they'd been given, it was all they had.

Even after all his speeches about right and wrong, Remy had to admit his fingers tingled with excitement. He was back to stealing for a good cause.

Life was coming full circle indeed.

He swung the small backpack he'd brought with his tools to the ground beside the window farthest from the street. From the bag, he pulled out his glass cutter. "Here goes." He started at the top-left corner and ran the device around the edge. "The hardest part is waiting to see if we tripped the silent alarm. Once we cut, we wait. Seven minutes. If the cops aren't here by then, we're safe."

"Sure thing, boss."

After laying the loose piece of glass on the ground beside him, he glanced back at her. "I think you're enjoying yourself."

She crossed her arms over her chest. "I'm not."

"Worried about Frank?"

"No. David and Mo are keeping watch. They won't let anything happen to him."

"Are you going to hate me forever for pushing you into this?"

"You didn't push me into this. Garner did."

"But you wouldn't even know he existed without me."

She knelt next to him. Even in the dark, chilly alley her warmth and scented lotion washed over him. The lemons reminded him of last night in Florida, of the closeness they'd shared—if only briefly. "I don't blame you, Remy."

He cupped her cheek, and the words just fell out. "I love you."

Her face went white. "What? You love me now?"

"I've known for a while, I just thought you should know now."

She sighed. "Your timing is lousy, Tremaine."

15

JADE PULLED BACK from Remy and stood.

The fact that they were breaking into a revered museum, risking their lives and reputations to take something that didn't belong to either of them, after which they planned to exchange it for her partner's life, and hopefully manage to trap a murderer in the meantime, apparently just wasn't enough excitement for her client.

He had to throw emotions into the mix.

"I'm guessing you're not going to rain kisses all over my face and return the sentiment," he said.

"Dammit, Remy."

"That would be a *no.*"

"Why are we doing this now?"

"We have seven minutes."

She glared at him. "You're trying to make me laugh. It won't work."

He straightened. "I'm very serious. I realize my timing's not especially convenient, but neither do I expect to be dismissed."

"Oh, hell." She paced away from him, then back. He drove her crazy. He was amazing. He challenged her. He comforted her. But he also forced her to look deep inside herself, where she didn't want to go, because it might make her realize her life, as she lived it now, was empty. "I can't do this now."

"Why not?"

She forced herself to meet his gaze. "I need you, but I don't want to."

"Dammit, Jade."

He was hurt and disappointed. Even in the dim light of alley, she could see those emotions cross his face. She didn't want to hurt him, but she didn't see how they could be together, either.

They were both too strong and opinionated. They valued their independence. They'd come together during a tense time. What did they really have to show for it?

Understanding. Laughter. Passion.

Completion.

She wanted to cry but was pretty sure she'd forgotten how. How could she be so sure how to handle each and every professional problem that ever slid across her desk and be so completely lost about one man?

"Let's go on our treasure hunt, then we'll talk," she said finally.

"Fine." He returned to his crouched position beside the window.

What was she so afraid of? Failure? Losing him? Compromising? Not being able to balance her demanding career with a personal life? Feeling too much? Being a woman and not just a bodyguard?

All of those. They all squirmed in a nervy ball of anxiety deep in her stomach.

She was a selfish, demanding person. Though she'd grown up watching her parents love each other, when they were ripped away from her, she'd been convinced she wasn't meant to have that kind of relationship. And after the NSA, she'd known she couldn't ever share herself completely with anybody else. She'd traded what might have been for revenge. She did it consciously. Selfishly.

He's like you. He knows you.

Maybe. But she didn't trust he would beyond the capsule of the week they'd shared.

I'm better off alone. It's what I always expected.

She knew when the seven minutes had expired because he simply held out his hand to her.

Lying on her belly, she slid feet-first through the small window opening and dropped to the cement floor below. He followed soon after, then they moved silently through a maze of cartons so huge the security staff must have decided there was no point locking them up. Who could ever get them out without front-loading equipment? Certainly not through the tiny window of vulnerability she and Remy had just slithered through.

They crept up the wooden stairs to the main floor. Jade kept close to Remy's back. She'd certainly been part of illicit operations before, but she'd always had a cover story and the backing of her government to fuel her. She'd been following orders and working toward a greater purpose.

Wasn't she now? To save Frank, she'd tossed every rule she thought she'd never break into the fire. How was what she was doing now so different from the life Remy had led all those years ago?

It's easy to stand on morality when you aren't desperate or furious. Or both.

No freakin' kidding.

Fascinated, she watched Remy pull out several tools, both mechanical and electronic, and work the door that led to the main floor of the museum. When it opened with a quiet click, she wasn't the least surprised but she was wildly impressed.

He pressed one finger to his lips, grasped her gloved hand, then led her down a narrow hallway. They followed a series of hallways, which contained offshoots of work rooms, break rooms and offices before reaching the edge of the lobby. There, Remy pointed silently at the camera that swept in an arc from the base of the main staircase to the front desk and back again.

She nodded, slid her hand to the butt of her pistol and prayed she wouldn't have to draw it. Reaching out, she squeezed his hand, knowing he was about to risk himself and create a distraction. If the local PD grabbed him, would the NSA protect him or wash their hands of him? Would his boss get the proof he wanted that Remy hadn't left his criminal past behind?

The risk he was taking for Frank was humbling.

They kept still and silent as they watched the eye of the camera move back and forth, then, as the camera moved away, he jerked her into motion. They ran up the stairs, then leaned back against the wall. They did that twice more before they came to the hallway where they had to separate.

His silver eyes darkened. He grabbed her by the back of her neck, pulled her close, then kissed her hard. "See you," he whispered just before he darted down the hall.

He was furious with her. She'd hurt him, and yet he continued to help and protect her while risking himself. She wouldn't let him down. She'd nearly assured Frank's safety, but their mission wasn't complete. They had to have that statue to close the circle.

Was it right or ironic that she would make that happen?

She timed her flight toward the San Francisco artists' gallery avoiding the arc of the security scan. Pausing outside the open doorway, her gaze locked on the bronze sculpture of

Remy's mother. She lay on her side, clothed in a slip-dress, hardened by the copper color that had immortalized her in youth. Her hair, somehow still glossy, was swept in front of her, dusting the floor.

She rested in the corner, instead of the center of the room, where Jade had imagined. But then, it was an insignificant piece in the art world compared with some of the others.

When she heard the rush of feet along the halls, she drew deep breaths but didn't move. She had to give the guards time to get to Remy. She had to hope he'd be slippery enough to escape as she snagged the prize.

When she felt certain the attention was on the other side of the building, she pulled a black ski mask over her face, darted into the room, grabbed the sculpture and stuffed it into the canvas bag she'd brought. It was heavier than she'd anticipated. She felt a weird sort of reverence as she clutched the artwork to her chest.

Breathing hard, listening for footsteps, she darted back downstairs and wriggled out of the cut-out window.

Please let him make it, she prayed, yanking off her mask and leaning against the building in the alley.

Moments later, she saw him race across the basement floor. It seemed to take forever before he was standing on the street beside her, but in essence had to have been only a few moments.

They clasped hands and raced down the alley and across two blocks, where the limo was waiting. Before Jade had drawn a decent breath, they were rolling through the streets toward the Marriott.

"Thirty minutes," she said, glancing at her watch. "We'll be lucky if we make it." She picked up her earphones and mic from the seat beside her where she'd left them earlier. "We got it," she said. "How's Frank?"

"On his way," David said. "Two goons are bringing him in a black SUV."

"Don't go after him until I give you the signal. We want the cops there. I don't want Garner squirming out of this one."

"Ten-four, boss."

"The next call won't be as easy," she said, turning to Remy, who'd pulled the sculpture out of the bag and was turning it over in his hands.

The statue was only about a foot and a half wide at the base and about nine inches tall. Though she knew nothing about art, even Jade could tell the detail in the woman's face and body was amazing. She had no concept of how somebody even began to create such a living-looking sculpture out of metal.

"Here it is," Remy said, pointing to a round hole on the bottom.

"What are you waiting for?" she asked, glancing at him, at the excitement and anticipation in his eyes.

"It may not even be in there. It could be hollow, or the painting could be a fake."

"Hand me the damn thing," she said impatiently.

"No, I've got it." He looked over at her. "It just feels strange, you know?"

His life was coming full circle. So many questions were about to be answered. "Yeah, I do."

He reached into his pocket, and she heard the seams rip as he retrieved the hidden ring. After he pried off the onyx in the center, he stuck the tiny key that was revealed into the hole on the bottom of the sculpture.

Click.

Jade caught her breath as Remy slid the base to the side. Rolled up inside the hollowed-out metal was a piece of canvas.

Remy removed it and used his hands to spread out the painting. It was a picture of an old farmhouse. Boring and ordinary.

"The overpaint?" she asked.

He examined the painting closely, then pulled an odd light device from his bag and ran it over the canvas. "I think so." Next from the bag came a small sponge. He touched it to the lower-left corner of the canvas. Colors began to blur.

She grabbed his wrist. "Are you crazy? What if there *is* a van Gogh under there?"

"The paint on top is watercolor. Our dear Vincent would have painted in oil."

"Oh." She let go of him but still winced as he continued dabbing gently at the canvas with the sponge. After a few minutes of careful work, one scrawled word was evident.

Vincent.

"I'll be damned."

"I need to get it to an expert to remove the rest," he said, his voice quiet and reverent as he continued to stare at the painting.

"We did it," she said in wonder. "We really did it."

"Thanks to you." Smiling, he kissed her lightly, then rolled up the painting and placed it in a protective tube he'd retrieved along with his other supplies.

"Garner is going to get eighty years for taking that thing," she said.

Remy angled his head. "What thing?"

"The painting. Trying to abscond with a real van Gogh. The guy will get barbecued by the press and the public." She rubbed her hands together. "I can't wait."

"No, he won't. I'm not turning over the painting to the police."

"Of course you are. Garner gets caught with the goods, we rescue Frank, Garner gets stuffed in the back of a patrol car and we open the champagne."

Remy reassembled the sculpture and returned the ring to his pocket. "If we give it to the police, the painting will wind up sitting in an evidence room at the Atlanta PD for years. It'll be caught up in miles of red tape and bureaucratic maneuvers. I won't let it happen. I'm compromising already by letting them have my father's statue, which will take me years of legal wrangling to get back."

Mouth hanging open, she stared at him. "You're not kidding."

"No, I'm not."

"But we need the painting for evidence. Don't you want to nail Garner?"

"The sculpture will have to be enough. One man was robbed and two men murdered for this painting. It's long past time something good came from its recovery."

She was still so floored by the realization that he was keeping the painting, that he most likely never had any intention of turning it over, she could hardly think straight. "What are we going to tell the police?"

"Everything—to a point. Garner blackmailed us into stealing a sculpture in return for Frank's life. He thought it contained an overpaint, but when we opened the base, it was hollow."

"But—"

"Even he doesn't know for sure about the painting. The only living people who know are in this car." He cupped her cheek in his palm. "It's going to stay that way. For now, anyway."

"We're double-crossing Garner," she said slowly, and for the first time she appreciated the irony and simplicity of

Remy's plan. But she saw one flaw. "He's going to know you lied eventually. You're not going to hang this in your rec room, are you?"

"No." Remy smiled. "And, yes, Garner will know I lied."

She licked her lips, turning the idea over and over in her mind. Surely, what they were doing was wrong. So why did it feel so right?

With a sweep of his thumb, he stroked her cheek. "Trust me, Jade. Trust me to do the right thing."

Though her stomach vibrated with nerves, she nodded.

He pulled her close and kissed her, slow and deep. It felt like a goodbye, and she realized in many ways it was. The case was all but over.

And so were they.

"Make your call," he said, leaning back.

She dialed Detective Parker's number on her cell phone. "Meet me right away at the Marriott Marquis lobby bar and bring the cavalry."

"You're going to be the death of me," he said, sounding tired.

"I'm gonna get you captain's bars, buddy. In fact, are you married?"

"Yes." Now he sounded confused.

"Any kids?"

"No."

"Good, then there's still time to name your first child after me." She explained how respected art dealer Peter Garner had confronted her and her client at a gallery showing earlier in the evening, that he'd kidnapped her partner and agreed to release him only if she and Remy brought him a bronze sculpture.

"There was a break-in at the High Museum a few minutes

ago," Parker said. "You wouldn't know anything about that, would you?"

"I refuse to answer that question without my attorney present."

"You couldn't just let us handle it, could you?"

"With my partner's life in jeopardy? No way."

THE SATISFACTION Remy felt watching Peter Garner being hauled away from the hotel bar in handcuffs was tempered by seeing the sculpture of his mother disappear into an evidence bag.

"Don't even *think* about getting it back before the trial," Jade said, obviously catching the direction of his stare.

"I'll try to restrain myself." He grinned. "Old habits are hard to break, you know."

The fact that a priceless van Gogh was stuffed under the seat of a rented limo while they leaned back against the car and waited for the paramedics' word on Frank's condition meant there was a great deal left unfinished with the case.

But it felt over.

"Nice job, Agent Broussard."

"You, too, Tremaine."

"I have to go to Washington and straighten out everything with the NSA. Will you be here when I get back?"

"No. I need to go home."

"Then I'll come there."

"I don't think that's a good idea right now."

Though she hadn't moved, he could already feel her pulling away from him. She'd trusted him with the painting, but her heart was still well guarded. "I love you, Jade."

She hunched her shoulders and stuffed her hands in her back pockets. "How do you know that? You've known me a week."

"It seems like forever."

"We're complete opposites."

"We did pretty well together tonight." He sighed when she remained silent. "I should think you, of all people, would be aware of how precious life is. It's too precarious to spend time questioning fate and wondering what the future holds."

"I'm *fine*," Frank said loudly. "I'm not going to the emergency room. I'll get sick there."

Even through his anguish, Remy smiled. David and Mo helped Frank off the stretcher, and they headed toward the limo.

Jade embraced her partner. "You're cranky. You need a nap."

"I need everybody to stop fussing over me. I'm fine."

She leaned back and smiled, the relief on her face obvious. "We'll get you home. David, hail a cab. Mr. Tremaine is taking the limo to the airport."

Obvious surprise slid across his face, but he nodded. He gave Remy a salute, and he and Mo walked away.

"You comin', J.B.?" Frank asked, his gaze darting briefly to Remy.

"Yeah. I'll be right there." She turned back to him. Her face was blank and emotionless. "I guess that's it."

"It doesn't have to be."

"We agreed to the length of the case. The case is over."

"Come with me," he said, holding out his hand.

She backed up. "I've gotta go to the station."

"They can wait."

She shook her head, dashed away a tear, then met his gaze straight on. "I'm better off alone."

"No, you're not. You're perfect with me."

"I can't," she said, turning away and breaking his heart.

He didn't watch her go. He ducked into the darkened limo. Laying his head back against the seat, he stared at the ceiling.

He'd gotten everything he wanted in life. He'd finally found his father, and the man responsible for his death would pay. His heart should be healed.

Instead it crumbled into a million pieces.

16

Lost Van Gogh Found and Auctioned; Proceeds Donated

Atlanta

Local art dealer Remington Tremaine has arranged for the donation of a sizable sum of money to the High Museum of Art and various San Francisco art societies from the sale of a painting by renowned Dutch artist Vincent van Gogh that was uncovered in a client's attic last month.

"I'd always assumed these sorts of things were just urban legends," the dealer said in an interview this week. "But apparently not."

The work, an oil on canvas, adds another blossoming orchard to the series that van Gogh painted in 1888 in Arles, a town in the south of France. It has been authenticated by several leading experts and is scheduled to be revealed to the public in two weeks here at the High Museum of Art. The museum has recently undergone a security overhaul to prepare for the already famous painting.

Mr. Tremaine declined to reveal his client's identity,

but the donations were made in the names of Paul O'Brian and Calvin Rothchild, both deceased.

The art world has been in the news quite a bit the last few weeks, as California art dealer Peter Garner was indicted on a variety of federal and state charges, including kidnapping, attempted murder, assault and theft....

JADE FOLDED THE newspaper she'd picked up at the airport in Atlanta and laid it on the seat beside her. From the side window of the cab, she watched the streets of San Francisco go by in a blur.

She'd chased the man across the country and all over the city in the last twenty-four hours. She hadn't slept. She should be exhausted, but she was too nervous to be tired.

If he wasn't at the cemetery, she was out of ideas.

After a month of working herself into the ground and wallowing in doubt, she'd woken up yesterday, rolled over and stared at the object on the bedside table just as she had every day since Charlie had given it to her.

But that day, she'd taken one look at the damn onyx ring and burst into tears. Which eventually turned into hysterical laughter, then back to tears.

Thank God she'd been alone. She'd never live down that pathetic scene if it had been witnessed by her team.

When she'd finally calmed down, one clear truth had become evident. She was scared.

She, Jade Broussard, former NSA agent, security specialist, bodyguard and investigator, who'd faced down terrorists, stalkers, politicians, bureaucrats, murderers and crazy clients was scared of falling in love.

She'd fought her feelings, denied them and ignored them.

All in an effort to protect herself. Her job—at which she was an expert—was to protect other people and risk herself. Why was she so sure she'd fail when the stakes were higher than they'd ever been?

I'm better off alone, she'd said to Remy.

What a load of bull. She wasn't alone. She had Lucas, Frank, David, Mo and Charlie. She had nearly a dozen other employees. She had a collection of loyal clients and associates.

After her parents died, she had cut off many of her emotions, but they'd all come back eventually. She still grieved, but she wasn't still traumatized. She'd healed. Her life had gone on.

Trying not to love Remington Tremaine was like trying not to breathe.

Impossible.

She didn't care that he used to be a thief. She didn't care that they seemed an unlikely pair or that they barely knew each other. She was tired of sticking to the straight and narrow path, of being afraid to love and suffer loss.

She was heading down a new, unfamiliar road and had no idea where it would lead. With Remy beside her, they'd find out together.

As long as he still wanted her.

After grabbing the ring, she'd hopped on the first plane out of New Orleans and flown to Atlanta, where a call to Remy's office had gotten her his answering service. He'd gone to San Francisco on business a few days before. So she'd boarded another plane.

Dozens of calls and a few thousand miles later, she'd gotten the name of his hotel, where the front desk clerk informed her she'd just missed him.

He could be anywhere—having lunch, sightseeing, swinging from the damn Golden Gate bridge.

The idea of the cemetery had come to her out of the blue. She knew from Frank that Remy had had his parents' graves moved to side-by-side plots next to the church and orphanage where he'd grown up. Sister Mary Katherine was most certainly proud.

As the cab pulled into the parking lot, she saw a lone figure standing in the cemetery and knew her hunch had paid off.

Heart pounding ridiculously hard, she paid the cabbie, then made her way to Remy. He didn't move as she drew closer, but she had no doubt he sensed her presence—his body stiffened.

"You dropped this in the limo," she said, holding up the ring.

He glanced at her over his shoulder. "I didn't drop it. I left it."

His face was blank, his eyes expressionless. She'd waited too long. He didn't want her anymore. He'd decided she was too difficult and stubborn.

She tried to swallow around her dust-dry throat. "Why?"

He lifted one side of his mouth in a grin. "So you'd have to return it." He grabbed her wrist and pulled her into his arms. "You sure as hell made me wait long enough."

Her heart finally settled back in her chest. She wrapped her arms around his neck and let his body warm hers. "Frank threatened to shoot me."

He kissed her jaw. "He told me that didn't work."

"It sunk in eventually."

In fact, remembering how Remy had risked himself for Frank had forced her to admit she loved him.

She'd tell him later about her journey. Right now she wanted to hold him and enjoy him, and tell him what she'd held back before. "I love you."

He brushed her hair back from her face and cupped her cheek. "I love you."

They shared a kissed filled with promise and hope, forgiveness and healing. Wherever they went in life they'd go together. She knew their parents would be proud of the choices they'd made.

"You know I had to fix the window at the museum," he said when he pulled back.

"Big deal. I had to fix their security system." She slid her fingers across his face. "I saw the story about the sale of the van Gogh. Calvin Rothchild?"

"He originally owned the painting."

"I figured."

He stared at the graves beside them. "I should have known him—my father. Why wasn't his name on the birth certificate?"

"They were never married. Maybe your mother was embarrassed. He obviously knew about you. Maybe she thought he'd come and get you later."

"He might have planned to. He just never got the chance." His eyes hardened. "Sean Nagel—his supposed friend—is to blame for that." He smiled as he looked down at her. "He wasn't a thief. I never realized how much it bothered me that he was until I learned the truth."

"And he loved you. He could have sold the painting himself, but he wanted you to have it."

"A few more obvious clues would have been nice," he said dryly.

"You've got a point there." She studied his handsome face and still could hardly believe he was hers. "Are you moving to New Orleans, or do I have to move to Atlanta?"

"I'm moving. I already bought a house."

She pressed her lips together. She'd see who got shot when she got her hands on her partner. He had to know about this.

"Though I can turn it into an office if you want to ask me to move in with you," he continued.

She smiled. "Deal."

"We'll have to get married eventually, you know."

Though her stomach jumped, that didn't sound nearly as scary as it should. "Yeah? Why is that?"

"Because of *her*," he said, nodding at someone behind her.

Jade turned to see a tiny woman, dressed in a nun's habit, standing a few yards away by the back door. She waved. "Sister Mary Katherine."

"The one and only."

"Well, you'd better get on her good side now, 'cause I'm taking you back to the hotel later and doing naughty things to you."

Heat filled his silver eyes. "Promise?"

"Promise."

She grabbed his hand, and they walked side by side into a brighter future.

* * * * *

Turn the page for a sneak preview of
IF I'D NEVER KNOWN YOUR LOVE
by
Georgia Bockoven.

From the brand-new series
Harlequin Everlasting.
Every great love has a story to tell. ™

There's no way for you to know this, Evan, but I haven't written to you for a few months. Actually, it's been almost a year. I had a hard time picking up a pen once more after we paid the second ransom and then received a letter saying it wasn't enough. I was so sure you were coming home that I took the kids along to Bogotá so they could fly home with you and me, something I swore I'd never do. I've fallen in love with Colombia and the people who've opened their hearts to me. But fear is a constant companion when I'm there. I won't ever expose our children to that kind of danger again.

I'm at a loss over what to do anymore, Evan. I've begged and pleaded and thrown temper tantrums with every official I can corner both here and at home. They've been incredibly tolerant and understanding, but in the end as ineffectual as the rest of us.

I try to imagine what your life is like now, what you do every day, what you're wearing, what you eat. I want to believe that the people who have you are misguided yet kind, that they treat you well. It's how I survive day to day. To think of you being mistreated hurts too much. If I picture you locked away somewhere and suffering, a weight descends on me that makes it almost impossible to get out of bed in the morning.

Your captors surely know you by now. They have to recognize what a good man you are. I imagine you working with their children, telling them that you have children, too, showing them the pictures you carry in your wallet. Can't the men who have you understand how much your children miss you? How can it not matter to them?

How can they keep you away from us all this time? Over and over, we've done what they asked. Are they oblivious to the depth of their cruelty? What kind of people are they that they don't care?

I used to keep a calendar beside our bed next to the peach rose you picked for me before you left. Every night I marked another day, counting how many you'd been gone. I don't do that any longer. I don't want to be reminded of all the days we'll never get back.

When I can't sleep at night, I tell you about my day. I imagine you hearing me and smiling over the details that make up my life now. I never tell you how defeated I feel at moments or how hard I work to hide it from everyone for fear they will see it as a reason to stop believing you are coming home to us.

And I couldn't tell you about the lump I found in my breast and how difficult it was going through all the tests without you here to lean on. The lump was benign—the process reaching that diagnosis utterly terrifying. I couldn't stop thinking about what would happen to Shelly and Jason if something happened to me.

We need you to come home.

I'm worn down with missing you.

I'm going to read this tomorrow and will probably tear it up or burn it in the fireplace. I don't want you to get the idea I ever doubted what I was doing to free you or thought the work a burden. I would gladly spend the rest of my life at it, even if, in the end, we only had one day together.

You are my life, Evan.

I will love you forever.

* * * * *

Don't miss this deeply moving
Harlequin Everlasting Love story about a woman's strug-
gle to bring back her kidnapped husband from Colombia
and her turmoil over whether to let go, finally, and wel-
come another man into her life.
IF I'D NEVER KNOWN YOUR LOVE
by Georgia Bockoven
is available March 27, 2007.

And also look for
THE NIGHT WE MET
by Tara Taylor Quinn,
a story about finding love
when you least expect it.

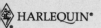
 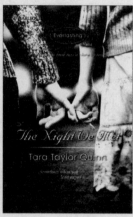

HARLEQUIN® *Romance*®

presents a brand-new trilogy by

PATRICIA THAYER

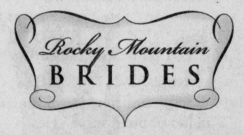

Rocky Mountain
BRIDES

Three sisters come home to wed.

In April don't miss
Raising the Rancher's Family,

followed by

The Sheriff's Pregnant Wife,

on sale May 2007,

and

A Mother for the Tycoon's Child,

on sale June 2007.

Romantic
SUSPENSE

Excitement, danger
and passion guaranteed!

USA TODAY bestselling author
Marie Ferrarella
is back with the second installment
in her popular miniseries,
The Doctors Pulaski: Medicine
just got more interesting...
DIAGNOSIS: DANGER is on sale
April 2007 from Silhouette®
Romantic Suspense (formerly
Silhouette Intimate Moments).

Look for it wherever
you buy books!

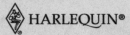

HARLEQUIN®

Blaze™

COMING NEXT MONTH

#315 COMING UNDONE Stephanie Tyler
There's a bad boy in camouflage knocking at Carly Winters's door, and she knows she's in trouble. The erotic fax that Jonathon "Hunt" Huntington's waving in her face—she can explain; how the buff Navy SEAL got ahold of it—she can't. But she sure wants to find out!

#316 SEX AS A SECOND LANGUAGE Jamie Sobrato
Lust in Translation, Bk. 1
Ariel Turner's sexual tour of Europe has landed her in Italy seeking the perfect Italian lover. But despite the friendliness of the locals, she's not having much luck. Until the day the very hot Marc Sorrella sits beside her. Could it be she's found the ideal candidate?

#317 THE HAUNTING Hope Tarr
Extreme
History professor Maggie Holliday's new antebellum home has everything she's ever wanted—including the ghost of Captain Ethan O'Malley, a Union soldier who insists Maggie's the reincarnation of his lost love. And after one incredibly sexual night in his arms, she's inclined to believe him....

#318 AT HIS FINGERTIPS Dawn Atkins
Doing it...Better! Bk. 3
When a fortune-teller predicts the return of a man from her past, Esmeralda McElroy doesn't expect Mitch Margolin. The sexy sizzle is still between them, but he's a lot more cautious than she remembers. Does this mean she'll have to seduce him to his senses?

#319 BAD BEHAVIOR Kristin Hardy
Sex & the Supper Club II, Bk. 3
Dominick Gordon can't believe it. He thinks his eyes are playing tricks on him when he spots the older, but no less beautiful, Delaney Phillips—it's been almost twenty years since they dated as teenagers. Still, Dom's immediate feelings show he's all man, and Delaney's all woman....

#320 ALL OVER YOU Sarah Mayberry
Secret Lives of Daytime Divas, Bk. 2
The last thing scriptwriter Grace Wellington wants is for the man of her fantasies to step into her life. But Mac Harrison, in his full, gorgeous glory, has done exactly that. Worse, they're now working together. That is, if Grace can keep her hands to herself!